BETTY

Brides of Williamsburg: A Sweet Colonial American Historical Romance

LUCY COLE

Chapter One

Betty Paca tilted her head to the side and let the fading sunlight play on the diamonds dangling from her ears. She admired herself in the reflection of her bedroom window's rippled glass, wondering when she might be able to wear them outside the house, if ever. No longer was she the fanciful little girl who could traipse around all afternoon, she was a woman, and as such, she should be thinking about marriage. The problem lie not in the marriage itself, but in the man. How did one choose the man she was to marry?

Betty's lips curled into a smile as she admired her reflection. She imagined wearing these exact heirlooms at her own wedding. It would be a grand affair. Her dress would be fit for a lady of the gentry, made with the finest fabrics, and perhaps dotted with gold. Betty would surely marry a rich, handsome man—

Williamsburg was full of them—she could have her pick. Women were in shortage in the colonies, and unless the men went back to England they were unlikely to find an abundance of female companions.

Unlike her cousins in England, she would insist on marrying for love just like her dear friend, Mary. She was not sure when she would meet the man she would marry, but she had all the winter season to find him, and longer if need be. There was no rush to find a husband for she had her father to support her.

Betty shifted her head and smiled again as the earring twinkled like a crystal in the Governor's chandelier. Heavy footsteps on the stairs made her start, heart thrumming in her chest. She quickly removed the earring and stuffed it back into its wooden box. If Father caught Betty handling her mother's jewelry again, he might actually fetch the switch he'd threatened her with the last time she'd been caught. Betty managed to get the box in place and pretended to be smoothing out the feather-stuffed pillow when her father stopped in the doorway, his blue eyes carefully considering her.

"Betty," he said, with a nod of his dark head. "You look more handsome than usual. Are you going somewhere?"

Betty looked down at her dress. It was borrowed from her dear friend, Sally, and too tight in the bust and hips, but it would be passable so long as she had no need to bend over. Her father hadn't enough money to replace frivolous things—as *he* called them—such as dresses and shoes every season.

Still, she considered herself lucky to be living in the colonies, instead of amongst the high society of England. Had she entered a ball in England wearing a dress two seasons old she would have been an outcast. Here, however, it was mostly understood that wealth was the result of a combination of good timing and hard work. Anyone could become someone of importance and station in the colonies. And it could happen at any time.

"Thank you, Father. Mary is to be married today and I will be attending. I spoke of it over breakfast. You must have forgotten. I have left a pot of stew over the fire and a loaf of bread under the cloth on the table." She turned to him, her hands resting on the top line of her skirts.

His eyes took her in briefly, looking over the soft pink and yellow dress, before darting around the room. Her father, normally still and stoic, could not seem to stay rooted to one place. Betty's eyebrows furrowed and she stepped towards him, hands extended. "Father, are you alright?"

"Yes. Yes, I have something to discuss with you, is

all," he said, grasping her forearms to still her, and perhaps to calm himself enough to speak.

She studied her father's face and her stomach fluttered at the way his eyes widened. She had seen that look once before. "It must be very important or very serious if you cannot stand still while thinking of it."

"We—"

His words broke off when the sound of knocking interrupted him. He forced a smile and twirled the two of them around so she was now standing in the doorway.

"Go to your wedding, my dear Betty. Enjoy yourself."

She frowned once again. "How am I to enjoy myself knowing there is something serious weighing on your heart, Father?"

He chuckled and gave her cheek a gentle sweep of his thumb. "Dear daughter, it is not so serious that it cannot wait. Go."

"Hello?" a sweet voice called up to them from below stairs. "Betty, it is Sally. Are you home?"

Betty glanced over her shoulder, and when she turned back to her father he nodded once more and shooed her away. "Mind your manners," he said. The stiffness of his lip meant he would not discuss what he'd begun to speak of until he was ready to do so.

And whatever it was, it seemed not fit for company's ears.

"A wedding, how truly romantic. Did you ever imagine that George and Mary would be married one day? I did..."

Betty and Sally were walking. Betty tried to hide how she clutched and released her hands as she thought of her father. Her eyes were on the dirt road ahead of them as they walked from one end of their stately town of Williamsburg to Palace Street, where Mary's future home would be. They passed by the market, now quiet and empty, and the stocks that were filled with criminals right outside the courthouse, yet she did not see a thing. Her mind was so busy worrying what her father would reveal that she hadn't heard a single thing her dear friend, Sally, said.

Sally studied her friend for a long moment, wondering if she were considering her question, before she realized Betty had not paid one iota of attention to it at all. She pinched Betty's elbow, pulling a gasp from Betty's lips. Her heated blue-eyed gaze turned on Sally, who stared at her with concern.

"My apologies, but you heard not one word of what I just said, did you?"

Betty's anger quickly disappeared, replaced instead with dread. "My mind is elsewhere."

"What is the matter?"

Betty shook her head and lifted her chin. She knew better than to bring doom and gloom to the surface. It was better to hide your negative feelings. Her father had always told her that you would catch more friends with smiles than tears. They'd had much to be sad about when her mother died, but the sadness only brought pity, and her father did not do well dwelling on the death of his wife.

"Nothing is the matter yet. We have a wonderful evening of dancing and drinks and food ahead of us. Let us not be bogged down in what we cannot control." Betty reached out for Sally's arm. Sally met her halfway and they each gave the other a squeeze on the forearm and a boisterous grin.

"I second those sentiments."

Sally grabbed Betty's other arm and swung her into a large circle. Betty laughed as she spun around, until she collided with something hard. She let out a little cry of surprise. It took Betty a minute to regain her senses and when she did, her chest grew warm from where it was pressed flat against that of a man. She was overwhelmed by the scent of him, his heat. Her cheeks began to flush as her eyes traced up his curves to the face of the man she almost knocked over.

Before her eyes could meet his, another hand tugged her away. "Miss Betty Paca, are you alright?" a masculine voice asked.

Betty blinked up at the new man staring down at her, amusement in his dark eyes. She put a hand to her cheek and took a step back, asserting modesty between them. Francis Garrett was one of Williamsburg's newest gentry. His father and mother had arrived in Williamsburg within the past several winters. His father had come to practice law, and Francis had yet to discover the talents he would charge a living for. Betty tilted her head back and quickly admired his dark onyx hair and his charming smile. "Mr. Garrett, yes, thank you. I am quite alright."

"This oafish gentleman did not harm you?" Frances asked in jest, indicating Thomas Murray, his peer with whom she'd collided.

Betty glanced in the direction Thomas had been, but he was now walking briskly away, his tawny colored hair billowing, his shoulders hunched ever so slightly. She looked back to Frances and smiled. "He did not harm me. How kind of you to inquire."

Frances nodded, a lock of his dark hair falling from its place beneath his hat as he brought her gloved hand to his lips. "A gentleman would do no less." He released her hand and regarded both Sally and Betty.

Betty glanced at Sally, regarding the way her friend's shining brown hair was always so neatly tucked beneath her cap. She turned back to Francis, intent on not feeling pity for her own wild black locks.

"Are you on your way to Mary and George's wedding?" he inquired.

Sally let out a wistful sigh beside her.

"Yes. Are you as well?"

He nodded. "Would you both care for an escort?"

Thomas sat inside his carriage and watched as Betty Paca and Sally Withers walked towards the wedding, one of their hands tucked into a separate crook of Francis Garrett's arms. He had known Francis for years, and he had never felt such distaste for him as he did in that moment. Since he'd left for Oxford the only woman who clouded his thoughts was Betty Paca. And when she'd looked at him just now, it was as if she had never before laid eyes upon him.

Thomas cursed himself for being such a fool. He

had been warned by Charles—the one good friend he'd made overseas during his studies—that despite how much money you owned, you could never truly own another person. And as much as you might pine for another, there was no guarantee they would pine for you in return.

He stepped into his carriage and pounded on the roof once he was safely settled inside. He was not looking forward to this event. If he had his way, he would not attend any social events at all. He much preferred the company of books and others who could hold an intelligent conversation. His mother had forced him to attend to both announce his return from England, and to find a suitable lady to court. His mother's words, not his own. He already knew whom he wanted to court. Or had, until she'd literally run into him on the street.

And yet he could not deny the physical sparks that charged through his body at their contact. When he'd looked into her clear blue eyes, he'd sworn he'd seen a hint that she felt the same attraction. But then she'd gone off with Francis, not giving the slightest glance backwards.

He tried to push it all aside. He had bigger problems than Betty Paca. His father was convinced he was truly dying. 'Truly' because this was not the first time his hypochondriac father had claimed his injuries were more extreme than they actually were. Thomas tried many times to convince his father that if he believed in the ailments so firmly, they might actually come true. When he'd left for England his father had been near death, both his father and mother had claimed. And four years later when he'd returned, his father was still alive and looked the same as when Thomas departed.

He supposed he should feel grateful his father was not a compulsive gambler or a man of otherwise loose morals, but it was still very difficult to fit into society when your father had no real place in it, other than to keep the doctor's pockets full. His father put his earnings into investing in other's projects, which had paid off thus far, meaning Mr. Murray did not have to be present and working. He was ill, or so he claimed, and spent most of his time holed up in his bedroom beneath his covers.

Thomas did not want that life. He was going to forge a new path. He'd secured himself an office and a few clients after he'd passed the Bar. He was now a licensed Virginian lawyer, and he planned to do everything in his power to make a good name for himself. He did not want to be known as "that unfortunate Mr. Murray's boy."

The carriage halted to a stop. Thomas leaned forward to find a precession of at least ten carriages ahead of him. He closed his eyes and took a few long breaths to calm his nerves. He recalled what Charles had often said to him: "Thomas, if you want to win the game, you oft have to begin playing first."

"I will play the game, Charles," Thomas mumbled to himself. But that did not mean he had to be happy while doing it.

Chapter Two

The wedding itself had been short and the applause rang loudly throughout Mary's receiving room. As the guests departed in different directions, some moving towards the center of the room to embrace and dance as the musicians started up, others towards the food being delivered to tables in the formal dining room, Betty and Sally joined their friends in the hall to formally greet each other.

They each embraced quickly, remarked on the other's dresses, and then the gossip promptly began.

"Did you see poor Anne's face through the ceremony?" Elizabeth inquired, her voice just above a whisper.

"Yes, the poor girl. I hope she won't lament long after her new brother-in-law. There are so many eligible men in Williamsburg and not nearly enough women," Lydia said, her hazel eyes alight with enchantment.

Mary was the first of their peerage to marry. And she'd married well, capturing the heart and hand of one of Williamsburg's most wealthy bachelors, George Bordly. Soon Mary would move out of her parent's home and into her very own estate. George would be serving in the House of Burgess, a very prestigious elected seat, and Mary would be swamped with social obligations and household duties. Before the next winter season, Betty expected Mary to be swollen with child.

Betty smiled at her group of friends and shushed them as Anne, Mary's sister and George's past courtship, approached. "Anne. Was the ceremony not lovely?"

"Yes," Anne replied, a false smiled pasted onto her plump lips. She tucked some stray red hair beneath her cap as if bored. "It was lovely."

"Who should we push to introduce you to first, Anne?" Charlotte asked as she grasped onto Anne's arm excitedly. Charlotte was the daughter of a prominent lawyer in town. Even if her father had not been a successful man, Charlotte would have a line of suitors. Her hair was raven colored, much like Betty's, however her eyes were dark, her lips fuller, and Betty admired her heart-shaped face, her own too square for her liking.

Anne jerked her arm from Charlotte's grasp. "I don't think I am feeling much above the weather. I may just go above stairs and lie down."

"Oh, no. You will enjoy the merriment. If not for yourself, then for all of us who do not want to see you sulking around so gloomily. Come, I'll sneak you some of the punch." Charlotte took Anne by the hand and their skirts swished gently as they walked towards the sparkling punch bowl in the middle of the hallway.

"I cannot wait to throw my sock at Mary this evening." Sally's brown curls bounced as she giggled.

"You don't honestly believe in that silly tradition, do you?" Elizabeth scoffed, tilting her pert nose into the air.

Sally shrugged her slender shoulders ever so slightly, and nibbled on the tip of her glove. "Tis better to hope than to be a grouchy madam such as yourself," she said with another giggle.

Elizabeth's emerald eyes rolled very improperly and Betty stifled a laugh. Her friends certainly kept her entertained. "Speaking of the bride," Betty said. "I should go seek her out and say my congratulations. Sally, I expect a full report when I return."

"On the eligible bachelors in attendance?" Sally inquired.

"No, silly, on the dessert selection," Betty countered. She swung away and headed towards the formal room, waiting for her turn to approach Mary. As she stepped closer, Mary excused herself from her new husband and took Betty by the arm, ushering her outside into the formal garden. Betty's stomach turned itself over. Why Mary had taken her away from her own festivities? Had she done something to upset her?

The gardens were down a line of steps, and the hedges made the large square plot more private. The crushed oyster shells were a pale white in the moonlight and contrasted very nicely with the bricks that lined the garden beds.

"Oh, but tis stuffy in there." Mary waved a fan in front of her reddened cheeks.

Betty stood in the middle of the garden with her friend, watching her pace back and forth. Again she was worried about her friend's actions. Was she upset about something? "Are you regretting the union?"

Mary paused. "Regretting the—" She shook the words from her mouth. "Nay, I regret only that we did not wait until the winter as is proper." Mary approached and gently put her fan under Betty's chin, lifting it until they met each other's eyes. Betty wondered if Mary could see the fear and uncertainty in her gaze. Could her friend tell she wasn't fully able to enjoy her wedding, because her mind was churning through the things her father might say when next she saw him?

Betty's gaze broke away first.

"What is wrong, dear friend?" Mary asked gently.

Betty was upset that she hadn't done a better job at hiding her wretchedness. She shook her head. "Nay, nothing. I refuse to spoil your wedding day."

"If you do not share, my wedding day will indeed be spoiled. You are trapped now. Please, share."

Betty let out a long sigh, struggling with what she would say to her friend.

"Oh. Tis about a man."

Betty paused, glancing up at her friend. Betty could open up to her friend about her unknown problems, or she could let her friend think the problem was about an unknown man. It would not be a lie to agree as it was concerning her father. "Yes," Betty said, quietly.

"Who is it you desire, Betty? James Greene? Thomas Murray? William Gates?"

Betty's mind flashed back to earlier, to the warm eyes and smile of Francis. And it was his name she muttered.

Mary chuckled and pretended to smooth some of

her auburn hair back into her voluminous bouffant, which was popular amongst Williamsburg's gentry women. "Well, that should not be too difficult. He is back from university. He is at the top of the prime marriage market as he has the means to care for any madam. He is a very close friend of my George. Would you care for an introduction?"

Betty shook her head, embarrassed by the thought of it. "Mary, he is above my station. He would have no interest in a merchant's daughter."

"Tsk. We are not English ladies and lords, Betty. I heard my George say there are murmurs of leaving the Crown after what it's done to our trade."

Betty did not care to speak politics, but even if she did, she knew speaking against the Crown could result in time in the stocks. She grasped her friend by her wrist and pulled her close. "Shh."

Mary chuckled and tapped her friend on the nose. "Do not worry, dear Betty. My point is... you should only fear if you cannot catch his attentions. You are very pretty with your ebony hair and your luscious lips. And your..." Her eyes dropped to Betty's bosom causing Betty to blush and step away.

"Mary, you are terrible."

"Terribly honest, my dear," she said, her willowy frame stepping in close again so she could speak frankly. "I have seen the way eyes drop. Even though it isn't polite, they do. I am not George's equal either, but here I am, married to him. The key is to make yourself irresistible."

Betty's fan pushed puffs of air to her heated cheeks. "How do you make yourself irresistible to a man of the gentry? Learn to cook well?"

Mary laughed loudly, so loud Betty's eyes went to the outer edges of the gardens, wondering if anyone would be concerned for her friend's mental well-being.

"Twas not overly funny," Betty said, her feelings slightly pricked.

"Nay," Mary managed, her throat still curling with amusement. "Cookery is but a small piece of it, but not nearly the whole. If you want to know how, I shall tell you..." Mary came in closer and wrapped a slender arm around Betty's petite waist, leading her back inside the grand two-story Georgian house.

"I was wondering where you'd gone to," George said. When he caught sight of his new bride, his lips curled into a smile. He glanced at Betty and waited for the introductions.

"Betty, George Bordly. George this is Betty Paca, one of my oldest and dearest friends." After pleasantries were exchanged, Mary's arm entwined with George's and she led him back towards the front room with Betty in tow. "Betty has an interest in

Francis. She was hoping we could introduce them. Perhaps he will ask her to dance?"

George looked surprised for a moment, but nodded. "Yes, of course." When his eyes met Betty's he tugged his lips up into a warm smile. "He would be lucky to dance with a beauty such as she."

Before introductions to Francis were made, Mary and George were pulled away by another couple who were slightly older than George. Betty returned to Sally's side amongst her circle of friends and they all commented on the fashions of the other ladies in attendance. Not long into the evening, Mary and Anne's mother started making introductions and before the sun fell, the dancing was in full swing. By the time the stars were fully lighted in the sky, Betty stepped outside, needing a break for her feet and some fresh air. She was sitting upon a bench when the crunch of oyster shells beneath boots sounded on the garden path behind her. Thomas Murray walked into the clearing, with his hands shoved deep into his pockets, his shoulders hunched once more.

"Mr. Murray," she said, announcing her presence as she stood.

His eyes widened in surprise at her presence looked surprised seeing her, and promptly held his hands up. "Please. Sit. I did not mean to disturb you.

I am sure your feet must be tired," he said, his voice forceful.

She smiled and sat back down once again. "Are yours not?"

He studied her silently for a moment, his eyes appearing dark in the lantern's glow. "No, they are not." He spoke softer this time, as if he were speaking with a scared, stray creature he'd come upon digging through the rubbish.

"How many waltzes does it take to satisfy your feet?" Betty replied, her eyes quickly taking in his suit. She had known Thomas Murray since childhood, but had seen very little of him since she'd left school shortly after her mother passed. The fine quality of his jacket and breeches spoke to his wealth, and even if she had not known his father was a man of gentry, his clothing would give him away.

"None. I do not dance."

She regarded him with a tilt of her head and a slight tip of her lips. "You do not dance? Why not?"

She waited for the answer that did not come. Instead, he changed the topic. "I apologize for being in your way. I often find myself in peculiar situations."

It took her a moment to figure out what he was eluding to, but once she did, she waved the comment away. "No need to apologize. I was the one, truly, who should be apologizing to you. Sally threw me around with all the force of a blacksmith wielding his hammer."

Thomas smiled at her comment, and his face changed completely for those few seconds. When he smiled, he was truly handsome. She didn't know what was wrong with her. She yearned for Francis and now Thomas?

Betty stood abruptly. She needed to retreat to a public place, there was no telling what would be whispered if someone caught sight of her out here unsupervised. And Thomas was not the man looking for a middling wife. Thomas had always been so serious. He needed someone equally as serious. Betty would surely drive him to drink or gamble with her desire for dancing and socializing.

"I should be heading back inside. Twas good to see you, Thomas. Good evening." She bowed her head and swiftly left him standing alone in the gardens.

As Betty cleared the door and began searching for her friends, Mary caught her by the arm, tugging her to the side. "Betty! Thank goodness. I have something for you." Before Betty could utter a word, an envelope was shoved into her pocket. "Don't open it until you are well alone and at home." Mary kissed her on the cheek and then she was gone again, her husband's strong hand on her elbow, pulling her towards the dance floor for a few more dances before they retired to bed.

Betty found Sally on the dance floor, twirling with some handsome young man. She stood by and watched for a moment, wishing she had Sally's free spirit. There was something about her friend. It had the gentlemen asking her for dances, fetching her something to eat or drink, or conversing with her until she laughed too loudly. She had no troubles securing company of the male persuasion. And Betty was the exact opposite.

Never had a man been interested in her, despite being what her friends called a natural beauty. Betty thought her long hair was too dark, her eyes too blue, her lips too large, her bosom too cumbersome. Her most endearing quality, she thought, was her desire to help. It often meant more work for her. Not only did she help her father, but she also tutored the little slave girl across the street when her mistress was out running errands, and helped the neighbor who was overwhelmed with six little ones and had no aid whatsoever. Her husband died of diphtheria while taking a journey to Richmond. Betty remembered the day when he did not return as expected. It was several weeks later when she found the announcement in the papers.

Her father. Her mind strayed back to him. She

wondered, again, what it was he'd wanted to discuss with her. She didn't have long to ponder before Mary and George announced they were heading to bed. Twas finally time! With the excitement she'd been lacking all evening, she followed her friends, who were trailing after the couple as they headed above stairs. Once in their bed, Betty and each of her friends removed a stocking.

"Ready?" Betty asked, looking across the row. Every one of them had a smile save for Anne. "And go!" They all pitched their stocking over their shoulders and with a squeal of delight Mary caught one. She held it up in victory. Betty blushed and covered her cheeks at the sight of her white silk stocking, the toe of it inscribed with her initials.

"Oooh, Betty, do tell. Who is the lucky man?" Sally teased.

Betty shook her head as they snatched back their stockings and put them on, watching George's friends take their places. A few made a jest about the smell once the shoes came undone, then before long, they were all throwing stockings over their shoulders as well. Thomas's gaze rested steadily on Betty as he pitched his over his shoulder. He did not even turn to see if it was caught. George came forth and pat Thomas on the back.

"Congratulations, old pal. You're next to be married. Perhaps Betty will let you court her proper."

Thomas's eyes fell from her as he retrieved his stocking. "Perhaps," he mumbled, before heading out of the bedroom in a hurry.

Curse the stocking ritual. Why was fate so cruel? Why was she consistently throwing Betty Paca into his path? Betty was not interested in him if her behavior this evening was any indication. As soon as she found herself alone with him she dashed away. Not that he could blame her. One touch seen by the wrong eyes would spread gossip of their faux courtship like wildfire, and they would then be stuck with each other. And he did not want to be stuck with an unwilling wife.

As soon as he arrived home, his mother came to help him out of his coat.

"Thomas, how was it, my dear?"

"It was a wedding, Mother. Love, laughter and punch all around."

"Love for you, my son?"

"Nay, Mother."

His mother let out a disappointed huff. "Thomas,

I do not believe you are even trying to find a wife. Do you not wish your father to be well?"

"I do, Mother. But my finding a wife, and his health, have nothing to do with one another."

She scoffed. "I know you believe that, but it is untrue. Can you not at least court one woman before the winter comes?"

He tightened his jaw, his irritation with his well-meaning mother growing. What if he did not wish to marry at all? What would she say to that? "Mother, if I promise to court *one* woman before the winter comes, would you kindly not speak of it again until next season?"

She handed his coat off to their servant as she grinned. "I would promise to, yes. Who will it be?"

"I have not yet decided, Mother."

"Come, you just spent hours with all the eligible ladies in Williamsburg. Surely one must have caught your attention."

Betty's name instantly came to mind. And it must also have come from his lips.

"Betty? Who is this Betty? Who are her parents?"

He closed his eyes tightly against her perplexed face. "No one. Forget I mentioned that name, Mother."

She squeezed his forearm tightly. "Oh, come. If

you do not indulge me I shall be forced to ask my friends about her."

And he could only imagine what they would say about Betty. She did not dress in the latest fashions, her hair was not ever pinned up properly, and her father was an unsuccessful merchant. "Betty Paca, Mother. Do not ask your friends about her. It would most likely be nothing but gossip."

She was quiet for a long moment, her eyes taking in his face. "The motherless child of the paper merchant?"

"Yes, that is her. However I believe she is hoping to court Francis Garrett, Mother."

"Why ever would she court Francis Garrett?"

"Does it matter? I do not wish to play second fiddle to him."

"Nay, I would imagine you wouldn't after what happened between the two of you during your first year at Oxford."

Thomas shuddered to think of it. He was but a young lad then, in a strange but familiar place. England was not completely unlike his colonial home, and yet in some ways so very different. Thomas was always a studious boy and that was how he found himself returning after dark to his dormitory one evening. He was halfway to his destination, when he heard a woman's scream coming from the darkness. It was followed by male laughter. Thomas quickly ran to the sound and stopped short at the sight of Francis and two others holding a maid against the brick exterior.

"What are you doing? Release her at once!" Thomas demanded. The three lads turned toward him and laughed.

"We are only doing as she wishes," Francis said. He turned to the woman and stared into her frightened eyes. "Are we not?"

With a whimper, she nodded in compliance.

"Release her or I shall tell the Dean of your repulsive hobby," Thomas warned.

Francis released the maid, but the other two did not. He came close to Thomas and lifted his lip in a snarl. "The Dean? Should I be frightened? Do you know who the Dean is? He is my uncle, so I will do as I please." Francis's gaze came to rest on Thomas's satchel. He snatched it from his hand and upended the contents onto the muddied lawn.

Thomas's fists curled as he stared at Francis's satisfied grin. Francis slammed the satchel into his chest, and Thomas grabbed ahold of it, then thrust it upon the ground. With determination, he stepped around Francis Garrett and outstretched his hand to the maid. "Come, you should not have to endure this."

The woman shook her head, her eyes filled with tears. She whispered, "Please, sir, tis not your place..."

Thomas was confused, his hand slowly dropped to his side. He did not feel it touch his thigh, however, before a hit to the back of his head stole his consciousness.

He had gone to the Dean the following day, his friend Charles by his side, but nothing came of his tale. Francis sat with the Dean and smirked as the Dean explained to Thomas that Francis was set to earn his degree in a few days' time so he could leave England and sail to the colonies. He had never been reprimanded for his actions, and Thomas had never forgotten Francis's lack of character.

Thomas's mother startled him from the memory, as she pressed a kiss to his cheek before letting him go. "Thank you for indulging me. I'm looking forward to hearing about the lucky woman you choose to court prior to winter, darling. Do not stay up too late. Good night."

"Good night," he said as he watched his mother disappear upstairs. It wasn't long before he followed her. He jotted the evening's events into a letter that he addressed to his good friend Charles, and set it onto the outgoing post pile. Perhaps his friend would have some helpful words for him.

Chapter Three

A knock woke Betty from her slumber. The wedding party had gone on until the early morning hours, and she'd barely had the energy to remove her clothing before crawling under her blankets.

"Betty, tis your father. Time to be up, the cock has long since crowed."

With a groan, she climbed from her bed. "I will be in the dining room very soon, Father."

Heavy footfalls retreated downstairs as she quickly dressed. When she entered the kitchen, her father was sitting at the table, an empty plate in front of him. He was clearly telling her, without words, he was disappointed she hadn't risen and made him food to break his fast.

"Do you have any errands to attend to? Food will not be ready in an instant."

When she approached, he pulled out a chair and motioned to it. "Sit."

She slowly sat. It was as if she were five, and about to be told it was wrong to lift her skirts in public. The fear bubbled up in her gut once more. "Yes, Father?"

He studied her for a moment, before dropping his gaze to the plate. He ran his fingers over the utensils, picking up the fork and then the knife. He twirled them around, all the while silent. His hesitation only made matters worse. She could think of several terrible things that may come from his mouth. Had he not been feeling well? Did the season not produce enough for them to continue renting on the prominent Duke of Gloucester Street? Was he going to marry her off to someone of his choosing?

"Betty, I do not know how to say this eloquently, so I will just come out with it. We are taking the Tiverton Ship back to England. It leaves in a fortnight."

Her mouth dropped open and she promptly shut it again. Twas not proper. "A fortnight? Father, that is rather sudden."

He grumbled and shook his head. "The decision had been made for months. I've arranged for us to live with your Aunt Tilda Hemmington in Essex."

"My Aunt Tilda? Mother's sister?"

"Yes. She has little ones and her husband recently passed. She is alone and struggling. She reached out to me, and I have decided to help her."

"Help her?"

He pressed his lips together as their stares clashed. She couldn't believe what she was hearing. Her father was going to *marry* her Aunt? Perhaps it wasn't as it seemed. Perhaps he would live under the same roof, but in his own bedroom, as a guest would.

"Marry her, Betty. Yes. I will marry her. She has agreed to have me."

Betty pushed herself from the table as if a fire was beneath her, ready to swallow her up. "You are taking me away from my home to marry mother's sister and care for her children? What of me, Father?"

His fist pounded the table, rattling the cutlery and stilling her in her tracks.

"You will help care for her children, Betty. You will help with the meals. And you will find yourself a farmer and you will marry him."

She opened her mouth once again to rebuke him, but her father held his hand up. "It has been decided, Betty. We leave in a fortnight. Say your goodbyes and pack your belongings into the trunk I place in your room this evening." His chair legs scraped the floor as he stood and stalked out of their home. Not that it would be their home for much longer, would it?

A swarm of emotions surrounded her at once. Fear mostly, because she had only yesterday regarded English society as snobbish. What life would she have over there being the governess to her three cousins? The tears stung her eyes as she thought about deserting her dear friends. Leaving them behind worried her most of all. She would not be as readily open to carrying on friendships after she took on the job of helping her Aunt with her home. Betty wiped at her eyes as she started the midday meal. Tears would only sour the stew, and if her father caught her crying he would rumble at her.

Crying does not get one what they desire, he always said. And he was right. But it did make one feel better for the moment. She paused slicing the carrot that appeared hollow in the middle. She held it up. The light shone through the empty cavity, and as she regarded it she thought it looked similar to a ring. A ring was exactly what she needed. A ring would be the answer to avoiding the misery that awaited her over the ocean.

She hummed one of last night's songs as she finished off the stew, and then went to her room while it simmered. Now her only problem was to figure out a way to catch a man. And not just any man would do. It would have to be a man of good station, one who could do without a dowry from her father. She did not want a man too many years her senior, she wanted to enjoy him and not be left a widow too early.

A little prick of worry niggled in her stomach. What if she could not find a suitor in such a finite amount of time? She pushed the thought aside. She had never before desired to marry a man for her father had provided her everything. This season was to be her first in Williamsburg, and it was just beginning. Eligible bachelors were beginning to swarm the streets in search of a woman suitable to be their wife, surely, she would find one who would meet her approval and desire her as well.

As she picked up her gown from the floor, an envelope fell from the pocket. She studied it, the beautiful scrawl of ink from her friend Mary's hand marked the front.

Recipe.

Curious about what recipe Mary thought was so important to slip into her pocket last evening, Betty opened it carefully, breaking Mary's old seal upon the back. She gasped as she began reading.

My Dearest Friend,

The past two months have been such a blessing to me for so many reasons. The least of not has been my engagement and marriage to my dearest husband. His eyes had been blinded to me but I set out to change that. And change it I did. Enclosed are the secrets to my success. The secrets I do hope you will be able to use to gain yourself a successful husband, a beautiful home, and a comfortable life.

The first secret... Make the gentleman take notice of you by whatever means possible, and instill in him the idea you are unavailable. Men want those things they cannot have. Make yourself difficult to acquire. Before you can indulge in the next secret, you must have fully acquired this step. You will know you are ready for the next step as soon as you have let him indulge himself with a secret hard-earned kiss. Do not let your gentleman earn this prize so easily. But also do not make it impossible for him to succeed. Tis a fine balance.

Betty sat down on her mattress, her dress and the letter on her lap. Make the gentleman take notice of you. Had she done that? Which gentlemen did she want to catch the eye of? Of course, she instantly knew. She wanted Francis Garrett. Francis was prominent and coming up in society, plus his family was well off so he would have no need for her to pay a dowry if he fell in love with her. Oh, but she had to act quickly. Mary had worked for months to get George to propose. Betty had a fortnight.

Francis was all she could think of as she went about her daily chores. And when she met up with Sally in the late afternoon for a stroll, she couldn't help letting his name spill from her lips.

"I want Francis Garrett to ask me to marry him."

Sally's boisterous smile was infectious. "Really? Truly? Betty! He is Williamsburg's most eligible. Have you begun courting?"

Betty's smile dropped slightly. "... Nay, not as of yet, but we will. Soon. I merely have to find a way to catch his eye."

Sally giggled. "Of course! Let us plan! You could arrive in his office wearing nothing but your shift."

Betty gasped and pulled Sally in close, covering Sally's mouth with her hand to keep her friend quiet. Betty glanced around and was relieved to see no one seemed to have overheard. "Sally, that is very improper."

"Proper is what you wish? How will he notice you then? Every girl in town is proper."

Betty quietly murmured, "What if I ask him to dance at the ball?"

Sally's eyes widened and she nodded excitedly. "Oh, yes!" She clapped her gloved hands together with excitement.

Betty wondered just how accepting he'd be of her

asking him to dance. There was nothing extraordinarily special about her. Perhaps if she stood out in some physical way it would sway him to make the move first and she would not have to. It would at least make it easier to catch other suitor's attentions in order to make Frances envious.

"And perhaps a new gown is in order."

"A new gown?"

"Yes. My old one is two sizes too small." And it would be her last ball in Williamsburg, she thought. She quickly shifted her mind away, lest she start crying in front of Mr. Charleton's Coffeehouse for the whole ton to see. "Will you come with me to the dressmaker?"

Sally's smile grew wider, which Betty did not think was possible. "I most certainly will."

Betty laughed softly and nudged her friend with her elbow. "Put those teeth away, Sally. You appear as devious as a cat with freshly sharpened claws staring, at a helpless mouse."

"I apologize for having such limited styles available. I'm afraid the ship from England has not yet arrived carrying my new supplies."

"Tis quite alright, I should've come dress shopping sooner."

"I suppose the other dressmakers were all too busy to help you on such short notice."

Betty's face heated with embarrassment. "I will not say that didn't have anything to do with my decision. But had there been options I would have sought out your shop no matter who had room in their schedule."

"Tis no matter, Miss Paca. I am just glad that you're here. Now let us see about getting you a dress."

Betty tried on many different styles and colors before she found the one that made both the shop keeper and Sally gasp.

"Oh, Miss Paca, this dress is perfect."

Betty stepped near to the window to see her reflection in the glass. The red of the gown certainly brought attention to her. She'd never seen herself in such a bold color. She shook her head. "No, tis too much."

"No, Betty, tis perfect," Sally echoed. "You do want to get his attention, do you not? No one would be able to tear their eyes away from you in that dress." Sally grabbed onto the large skirt and pulled it aside to admire the silk fabric. "And I have heard it said that red is the color of seduction."

Betty blushed and shushed her friend. The dressmaker, Madam McDowell, chuckled softly as she nodded her head. "Tis true. Who are you trying to catch, my dear?"

Betty's smile was soft against the blush of her cheeks. "I dare not say lest it not come to fruition."

"A superstitious girl. Curious that," the dressmaker said. "Come, let me take your measurements so I can begin. I will send the bill to your father?"

The debt would surely shock him. It would be best if he did not know until after the ball. "No, I shall take it with me and return with your payment within the fortnight."

Her father was not one to skip on his debts and so the dressmaker agreed. "I will have the dress delivered to your residence on the morrow, you will have plenty of time to dress before you must leave for the ball. Oh, and Miss Paca?"

Betty paused in the doorway. "Yes, Mrs. McDowell?"

The dressmaker paused, a cautious smile on her lips. "Good luck catching a husband, my dear girl, but do choose wisely. Not all men with money are worth giving your affections to."

After parting ways with Sally, Betty's merriment over the dress had begun to fade. Her father would be furious when he discovered what she'd done. He would be furious she was trying to prevent herself from joining him in England, and most of all for compiling a debt at Madam McDowell's shop.

She also could not help but think of the dressmaker's parting words. Was she so desperate she would marry any suitor with money? Could Mrs. McDowell see the desperation on her face? Betty had not even considered the idea she might choose incorrectly and be stuck with the man until death parted them. Was Francis Garrett one of those men? Surely he could not be, for he was acquaintances with many delightful men, including Mary's husband George. George and Mary surely would not allow Betty to be taken by the devil—they would have her best interests at heart.

The evening sun was close to falling as she passed by the printing office.

"Miss Paca..."

She turned at the sound of her name as Thomas Murray jogging toward her. She paused, holding her basket of goods in front of her skirts. When he stopped beside her and offered a bow, she gave him a curtsy, ignoring the fluttering in her stomach. Perhaps she had eaten something rotten.

"Mr. Murray." She met his gaze with a polite smile. "How do you do?"

"You dropped this," he said, holding out the debt slip.

Her gaze dropped to the slip. Now he knew how much her new dress cost and that she hadn't the money on hand to pay for it. With flushed cheeks she took the note and stuffed it into her pocket. "Twas very kind of you to return it."

He nodded his agreement and stood awkwardly, staring at her for a long moment. At first she took the opportunity to stare back. She had never noticed before how gold his eyes appeared. Or how symmetrical his nose was. As his eyes dipped to her lips and stayed fixed there, a breath hitched in her throat. Had crumbs from her breakfast stuck to her lips?

When her eyebrows furrowed, he cleared his throat and turned away, not even leaving her with a polite goodbye.

When she was sure he was gone she turned on her heel and started up walking again. Secretively she swiped at her lips, but felt no resistance. Why had Thomas stepped away so quickly? Was he ashamed to be seen talking to a woman from the middling class? Was he embarrassed on her behalf?

With a shake of her head, she let it go and continued home.

Once inside, she put her goods down and promptly went to her room. She winced as her toe slammed into the corner of the large trunk that had not been there when the sun came up. Gingerly, she walked towards her lamp and lit it, then stared at the trunk with spite. "You will not receive any of my things. Mark my words. Not until I will move you into Francis Garrett's house."

"Betty?" Her father's voice carried above stairs.

She stuffed the debt under her pillow and carried her lamp below stairs to start supper. It would be a long day tomorrow as she waited for her dress to arrive. It was going to drive her mad. Tonight she would plot how else to be sure Francis Garrett noticed her, but she was sure she would come up dry. For if the dress did not do it, she was not sure what could. "Coming, Father."

He had nearly kissed her. He could not believe his stupidity. It was as if all rational thought had left him and he became addle brained while staring at her, which made absolutely no sense at all.

He hadn't had a second thought about running after her. He'd seen her drop something, picked it up off the ground, and ran to her as if he were a hungry man running after a half dead deer.

He disgusted himself.

Thomas made his way back to his office. He had only gone out to grab a bite to eat at the tavern and see if there was any gossip he could turn into business. He'd found something of a buried treasure chest.

Mr. Purcell, a local shipman, had been found dead in his home a few days prior. It was rumored his wife had done it and while no one could prove it, there was good reason to believe she had, since Mr. Purcell made a habit of beating his wife.

After grabbing his things from his office, Thomas headed down to the gaol. The gaoler was in the brick lined outer edge of the gaol, serving the prisoners their food through the iron doored slats when he arrived, and smiled when Thomas approached.

"Another lawyer to see Mrs. Purcell? She won't speak to none of you," he said.

"I just need a few minutes, Mr. St. Clair. A few minutes and I promise I will not return to you about Mrs. Purcell again."

Mr. St. Clair sniffed loudly as he assessed Thomas. "When I've finished serving them twill be time for roaming. If she wishes to come speak with you through the door, she shall."

Thomas nodded and stepped away from the gaol. The longer he spoke with Mr. St. Clair the longer he would be standing there. There was a reason the gaol was on the edge of the town, away from the richer residences. The chamber pots here were not emptied as often as they should be and on top of that, some of the prisoners thought it more satisfying to use the floor instead. The smell emanating from inside was horrible. He did not envy Mr. St. Clair in the least. No doubt his house, which was attached to the gaol, smelled equally as bad, especially in summer.

When the yard was open and Mrs. Purcell came out to unstiffen her legs, Thomas approached the bars. "Mrs. Purcell, I wish to speak with you. My name is Thomas Murray. I have returned to the colonies from England. I attended Oxford, and I would like to speak with you of your innocence."

"Piss off," came a male voice from inside one of the cells. "She rammed him through with the knife, she told us all."

"If that is true, Mrs. Purcell, then there is no hope for you. You will be hanged. But if you are innocent, I can help you. I will do everything in my power to keep you off the gallows."

Mrs. Purcell's head lifted and she glanced at

Thomas as if he might actually be telling her the truth.

"You have suffered enough at the hand of your husband, Mrs. Purcell, you need not suffer any more. Let me help you."

After a long moment of staring at him, she approached the bars and whispered. He strained to hear her, turning his ear to the metal.

"I was there, Mr. Murray, but I did not murder my husband. It was another man. A man of the gentry."

"Who was it, Mrs. Purcell?"

She shook her head. "I will not tell. If I do he will surely have my life as well. I am doomed, Mr. Murray, and that is why I have refused a lawyer. I die at the gallows, or I die at the hand of the gentry. Either way my life is lost."

"Mrs. Purcell, I can protect you."

She shook her head. "I am safest in here, Mr. Murray."

Thomas did not have much choice in the matter if she did not wish to be represented. A deep burning in his stomach twisted at the thought of someone of his station taking advantage of the poor, as had been done with the Purcell family.

"If I have evidence against this man I can present it to the judge, the court."

"There is no hope, Mr. Murray. Tis better if you

accept it as I have." She smiled sadly before padding away.

"Twenty more paces, Mrs. Purcell," Mr. St. Clair yelled to her from beside Thomas. "Good try, Mr. Murray."

Thomas nodded but he was not going to give up this easily. Mrs. Purcell did not deserve to be convicted of a crime she did not commit. He would try as hard as he could to find justice for her.

Before it was too late.

Chapter Four

The red dress had been laying on her bed for the better part of the day. She'd scolded herself several times throughout the dinner preparation as she found herself inching towards the stairs. The dress could wait, the dress *must* wait else her father would catch her defiance in time to prevent her from going to the ball. And the ball was integral to her plan. So no matter how badly she thirsted to slip into the crimson silk, she would wait.

She'd been contemplating all day of what distraction to offer her father so he would be away from the house while she prepared for the ball. At supper, she approached the topic.

"Father, I was hoping for a larger trunk."

He grunted and then blew to cool his stew. "Betty,

the trunk is large enough. What does not fit, does not travel."

"Are you sure you could not make an allowance? I am doing as you bid, I am going with you to England. The least you could do is allow me one little luxury."

He paused, stew to his lips as he studied her. Thoughts circled behind his eyes. She hoped he would be merciful and go along with her plan, when finally he shook his head as he hung it in defeat. "Fine. I will fetch a larger trunk in the morning."

Panic rose in her chest. That was not how she'd planned it, and she had no rebuff as to why he should not go tomorrow morning. "Could you not fetch it now?"

"Betty, you have a ball tonight and the shops are near closed for the day."

"I know, but I was hoping to know how much would not fit so I may know what I need to offer my friends. Would you please go fetch one this evening?"

He set his spoon down loudly and sat back in his chair. "Anything else you desire while I am out? A kitten? A puppy? Two pounds of sugar and spices?"

She smiled softly. "No, Father. A larger trunk is all I require this evening."

He grunted and resumed his eating. He slurped his stew loudly, very ungentlemanly like. She huffed. He huffed in return.

After he was gone, she hastily cleared the dishes from the table and went to her room. She quickly made up her hair before finally starting on her dress. It would take her a good part of an hour to slip into the many layers that dressing for the ball would require.

When she was finished, she approached the glass of her window, her lantern in hand to illuminate herself. The gown dazzled and glowed, shimmering in the low light. Sally had been correct. Every man and woman at the ball would be staring at her this evening. She was both looking forward to it and dreading it at the same time.

Movement in the street beyond the window caught her eye. She saw a man below, bundled in a black cape and a pointed hat, heading down the street towards the south edge of town where the Foster's ball would soon be accepting guests.

She slipped on her red silk shoes, tightened the straps, and stood up straight. She regarded herself once more in the mirror and shook her head. Something was missing. She knew what it was as soon as her hand went to her chest. She had no sparkle. With soft fingers, she tapped her collar bone as she considered her options.

She was already going to be in trouble for buying the dress, and for her scheme to avoid leaving

Virginia. If Father found her in the jewels now, there was nothing he could do to punish her worse than what he'd already done. And perhaps he wouldn't notice their disappearance at all, and she could slip them back into place before he became aware they were missing.

It was decided. Betty slipped from her room into his and found the jewels in the same spot they'd been for the past fifteen years. With indulgent fingers, she reached in and pulled out the gorgeous ruby and diamond necklace before clasping it into place. It took her a few tries, but once she was sure it was secure, she reached in again and pulled out a matching diamond bracelet. This was trickier to clasp. Her full focus was on getting it secure, when her father's footsteps came from below stairs. She gasped and stuffed the jewelry box back into its secret position. His loud footfalls on the steps nearly matched the beating of her heart.

She tried to make it to her bedroom in time, but her father's thunderous voice stopped her dead in her tracks. "Betty! What are you wearing?"

She turned slowly, her cheeks burning with embarrassment and shame. "A dress, Father."

"Where did you acquire said dress? Did you borrow this one too? It looks brand new."

She swallowed hard, her eyes staring steadily on

the floor. She wasn't ready to confess to him everything. But again, what was the worst he could do? She lifted her chin defiantly and stared her father in his angry, dark eyes. "It is brand new. My other gown was much too small. My bosom was indecently shown, Father. I was gaining too much attention for improper reasons."

He scoffed. "And you think this sin colored dress will bring you less attention?" He shook his head. "I thought you were ready, Betty. I thought you were grown, but this shows me you are still but a child. Go into your room and remove that dress at once. Hopefully the milliner will refund the debt if you return it unworn."

"I'm not going to return the dress, Father. I'm going to wear it tonight to the last ball I'll attend in Virginia. You're stealing me away from everything I know so you may play house with Mother's sister. And you expect me to go along with it with a smile on my lips. But I will not. I am not a child, I am a woman. And I will prove it to you, Father. Just wait and see."

He was silent for a long moment before he burst into laughter. He doubled over and his cheeks were so red with mirth, she was concerned he was perhaps ill. But then he stood up straight and wiped at the tears that had escaped his eyelids. "Oh, Betty. Sweet girl..." He nodded to the jewels she wore and quickly his mirth disappeared, replaced by a bitter tone. "I hope you enjoy the dress that has cost you your mother's jewels. Enjoy them tonight for you will never wear them again. Do not let a man under your skirts, Betty, I will not be standing by to make sure he weds you. You obviously no longer have a need for me. Your trunk, which I now suspect was just a ploy, is below stairs. Good evening." With a nod, he disappeared into his bedroom, closing the door behind him, leaving her staring after him in the hallway.

She huffed as she returned to her bedroom and grabbed a cape. She wrapped it around herself, covering most of her dress, before heading onto the dark streets for the ball. The beginning of her second ball of her first season was not as giddy as she had expected, but she was determined not to let her father's punishment cloud her evening. She would prove her father wrong, and get Francis Garrett to marry her. Armed with Mary's excellent advice how could she fail?

Chapter Five

Nerves were all she could feel as she was greeted by the Foster's slave and butler, dressed in a modest blue dress covered with a crisp white apron and matching cap. Another slave, dressed the same, showed Betty to a side room where she discarded her cape. Betty held her chin high as she entered the grand dining room and joined her friends who were standing to the side. The candlelight flickered a good two feet above their heads, making all the gold in the room glitter like stars as the sun's light quickly faded.

Sally grabbed a hold of Lydia's arm as Betty approached. Lydia's mouth was agape as she took in Betty's new red dress. Betty's chest tightened with glee as she paused to give a little twirl in front of her circle of her friends.

"Betty. That dress is..."

"Yes," she said softly, dropping her eyes and smoothing down the red silk. "Is anyone looking?"

"Everyone is looking," Lydia confirmed.

"And Francis Garrett?" Betty asked, raising her gaze slightly, hope alight on her cheeks.

Lydia snuck a peek around Betty's form and then met her eyes with a shake of her head. "Nay. He is not looking at you."

Betty's lips puckered into a frown and her shoulders dropped. "Are you certain?"

Lydia's sky blue eyes danced around the room. "Yes. Undeniable. He is speaking with George near the punchbowl.

"George?"

"Yes."

Betty let out a deep sigh and finally turned around, putting her back to the wall so she could assess the scene. Indeed, Francis was standing near the punch, deep in conversation with George. Mary was beside them, half listening as she scanned the ballroom. When she spotted Betty, her eyelids widened and she gave her a sly grin. She rolled her eyes toward Francis and lifted her shoulders. Betty shook her head and looked away.

This was not going to go as she hoped. Her

chance to stay in Virginia was quickly dwindling, to the sound of her father's laughter, which made her stomach swirl.

Lydia leaned in close and nudged her. "Betty, tis my belief Mary would like you to join her by the punch bowl."

Betty glanced at Mary, dressed in a very fine green and gold dress, sternly beckoning her over with one finger.

"Of course. Excuse me."

She could not ignore the feeling of eyes upon her as she glided as gracefully as she could muster across the large room. Betty Paca was finally being seen by everyone but the man she coveted to see her.

"Betty!" Mary said boisterously as she held onto Betty's forearms and gently pulled her in for cheek kisses.

"Mary." Betty nodded to her friend less enthusiastically. "How is your evening?"

"Spectacular." She heaved her close and murmured into her ear. "Spectacularly boring. My husband has yet to dance with me because he is debating with Francis. I would not have called you over except for your attraction to him. I was hoping we could mutually benefit from this diversion. Query him to dance."

Betty wheezed. "Pardon?" Mary furnished Betty a glass of punch and then thrust her squarely towards Francis. She gasped as she tripped on the lace of her skirt and tumbled towards the floor. Strong arms were around her before she met with her descent, and she was drawn upright. Her punch had spilled on both her dress and Francis's breeches.

Her gaze plunged and her cheeks flushed with humiliation. "Oh, I am terribly sorry."

Francis assessed the damage. He grinned as he gently swiped at the wet spot with the back of his hand as if a fly were buzzing about. "Do not worry, tis but a pair of breeches. A bit of coin will remedy the problem." Her cheeks burned. A great bit of coin would be needed to replace the silk. "Are you alright?"

She gave him a slight nod, words unable to dispense from her lips when he stared down at her. He was finally seeing her. She searched his face, wondering if he desired to kiss her.

"Let us go clean up so we can return to the festivities." With a wink, he gently turned her around and ushered her towards the back hallway, where the slaves could fetch them some wet cloths. It wasn't until she asked for two towels and received an odd look, did she turn to Francis who was no longer behind her.

She stood on tiptoes and saw him bent down,

Grace speaking into his ear. Whatever she said made him laugh loudly. Her hand rested on Francis's outer coat and Betty's heart seized with panic. She was going to lose her chance. Her eyes landed on a familiar face and her determination renewed.

She stalked back into the ballroom, the sticky mess from the punch forgotten for the moment. She pushed herself between Francis and Grace, and grabbed Thomas, who was standing directly behind them. She took his hand in a very improper way and tugged him towards the dance floor. Luckily, he did not resist.

With her hand on Thomas's shoulder, her gaze met with Francis's. She hurried her attentions back to Thomas and she offered him a minute smile. "I hope you do not mind dancing with me," she said delicately.

"I did warn you that I do not dance," he said as he put one hand politely onto her back, the other holding hers.

"Everyone dances. Just follow my lead." She waited for the right beat in the music to start, glancing at Francis once more. He was still observing her, rapt. She secreted the smile that appeared upon her lips, and turned her attention once more to Thomas, whose hands were unexpectedly sturdy and warm. Fluttering twirled in her stomach and for a moment she was distracted.

"I will lead," he said as he took command, and began dancing with her across the floor. She was startled and spellbound with his skill. After a few dizzying spins, Betty focused fully on her dance partner. She grew anxious in his arms, her body heating under his touch as she stared up into his serious face. She attempted to distract herself from the unfamiliar discomfort by engaging Thomas in conversation.

"You are very handsome when you smile," she said.

"You have not seen the whole smile just yet," he retorted, holding his lips firmly in a straight line.

"Ah. Do you save that for special occasions?"

"Special company," he countered.

"And I am not special enough? I am hurt."

"I would feel terrible if I believed it were actually true, but I know you Miss Betty Paca, and you are not easily hurt."

The familiarity with which he spoke made her heart hammer in her chest. "Perhaps you do not know me as well as you think you do."

"Perhaps. But perhaps I do know you as well as I think I do. I think there is something weighing on your heart, Miss Paca. Do you wish to share with me why you do not smile with all of your lips?"

Her eyelashes fluttered as tears threatened to break through. How could he see to the depths of her? She regarded him carefully, taking note of the way he held her, as if she would float away if he let go.

"No. But there is something lonely about *you*, Mr. Murray."

"That is hardly a secret, Miss Paca. You are stating facts that are public knowledge."

"Why you are lonely certainly is a secret. Why are you not married or courting?"

"Perhaps I have not found a woman I wish to court."

She pushed away the stab of disappointment his words brought.

"Or perhaps I have other pressing matters on my mind, Miss Paca. Like my new career. Or perhaps I have found someone I wish to court, but have not made a move yet."

"Why would you hesitate? This is not chess, Mr. Murray."

"Perhaps I am afraid."

"Afraid of what?"

"Afraid she may have designs for someone else, or may not wish to be married to me. I believe every woman and man should have a choice in matters of the heart."

Betty's gaze flicked to Frances, who was drinking

a cup of punch and leaning down to listen to another thing Grace had to say. Betty's chest gave a squeeze of displeasure. Francis's attention was dropping away so selfishly, Betty did what she felt in her heart would draw attention. With shaking hands and a heart beating so hard she may perish, she slipped her hand to the back of Thomas's neck and drew him down for a kiss. The instant their lips touched a spark of desire surged through her. That tickling in her gut shifted into a full blown punch of longing, and for a moment everything around her was forgotten. His hands tightened around her, drawing her in closer. Everything disappeared except Thomas, and the feel of his body pressed to hers.

Her breath caught in her throat as Thomas sharply pulled away. He looked panic-stricken, eyes wide with fear or humiliation, before he bowed and left her standing in the middle of the dance floor. All at once, the murmurs amongst the guests surrounded her.

She stared after Thomas, stunned. She had experienced nothing like that in her twenty years. Had he felt it too? Is that why he'd left in such a hurry? Or was it the indecency of her act that had surprised him? Had his lips returned her desire? Or had she merely imagined them doing so?

Her lips were still tingling when Francis

approached her. "You look like you need saving. A woman being left on the dance floor after kissing a man might easily die of embarrassment," he said as he took her into his arms. They did not stir feelings in her as Thomas's had.

She looked up to him and smiled faintly. "Thank you."

"Certainly. Though I do wonder why he walked away in such a hurry. Could it be your kiss was so terrible?"

Francis was trying to make light of the kiss and the verbal teasing did the trick, enticing Betty's thoughts to the present. She clutched Francis's shoulder tighter to illustrate her disdain. Perhaps the pleasure of her kiss with Thomas was a common experience for a woman. She had kissed no other man, how could she know? Her smile deepened as she retorted, "I should hope it was not. But on the off chance it was, would you care to give me lessons?"

Francis chuckled, his dark eyes twinkling as he stared down at her. "Perhaps. But not in front of all of Williamsburg. There will be talk, and if you are such a terrible kisser I do not wish to be stuck with you."

She tittered in return, offering him a shake of her head.

Curse you, Betty Paca.

Once again she had caused him to act foolishly. He had been walking unhurriedly amongst his peers, observing vigilantly every last one of them on the off-chance something was amiss and he would uncover the true murderer of Mr. Purcell. He had lingered when he'd heard George and Francis conversing about the Purcell murder and the property that would be left behind once Mrs. Purcell was hanged.

It was a rather unexpected topic to be discussing at a ball. He had stepped closer to be sure it was as he'd thought he'd overheard, when Betty approached, stumbled, and spattered her tipple all over Mr. Garrett. Thomas had hurriedly moved away, not, he tried to convince himself, because he was upset with Mr. Garrett's hands on Betty, but because he did not want to be caught eavesdropping on the previous conversation.

He had come full circle at the exact moment Betty had clutched onto him and yanked him to dance. He should have declined the invitation, but he hadn't been able to let go once she was in his arms.

And then, when he thought he'd gained the upper hand on the situation, when he had finally started to open up and hint at a courtship with her, she had done the unthinkable and kissed him. He had to admit the kiss had affected him. It would be a long spell before he could forget the sensation of her lips on his and now he would live every day knowing kissing her made him feel so... complete.

He'd had to walk away from her before he'd entirely lost control. It was unhealthy, the way she caused him to react. It was improper, the way he wanted to throw her over his shoulder and take her home to his bed. He knew he would never do such a thing without the woman's consent, but the thought had occurred to him.

Thomas blew out a hot breath as he stood out front, waiting for his carriage to circle around and collect him. He glanced over his shoulder and when his eyes fell on Betty and her new dancing partner, Francis Garrett, his chest tightened. They looked quite well together, both dark of hair, both grinning and gay. Though it pained him, he forced himself to memorize it. Perhaps if his brain realized Betty desired Francis then Thomas would be able to put her from his mind.

Then again, if Francis or George were the guilty party to Mr. Purcell's murder, Betty may not be safe. He shook his head and climbed into the carriage as it stopped. He could not concern himself with such tonight. He had to prove, one way or another, who was actually guilty of the murder before he went around pointing fingers and assigning guilt.

Betty managed to dance endlessly at the ball. If it was to be the last ball she ever attended in Virginia at least it had ended on a happy note. Her dance card had never been so full. The dress had most definitely been a success.

With her cape donned around her shoulders, she made her way onto Nicholson street. Most were drunk and returning to their homes, some were still inside dancing. Some were inside smoking and talking of politics and the King. With her hand tucked into the crook of Francis's arm, they crossed the road and began the walk back towards her home.

"You were the most delightful looking woman at the ball this evening," he said, looking down at her.

"Thank you. Even more delightful than Grace?"

"She could not hold a candle to you."

Betty smiled in spite of herself.

"That pleases you."

"Of course it does. Would you not like to hear you were the best at something?"

He shrugged his shoulder. "I am the best at many things. Kissing being one of them."

She laughed. "I have not kissed you so I cannot tell if this is truth or not."

His eyes seemed to glimmer as he met hers. "Would you care to feel my lips upon yours?"

They had stopped walking at some point and his hand moved to her hip, pulling her in close to his body. The sound of crickets and the flickering of the lamp lights surrounded them. She said nothing and did not have to, for his lips were dropping towards hers. She held her breath and braced herself for what was to come. And then the shrill female laughter pulled them apart and Betty was grateful. She had quickly forgotten the first part of the rule. She should not make the kiss so easy.

"Perhaps the middle of the street is not the place for it," she said.

"Perhaps not," he replied as she continued to walk beside him.

Disappointment curled around her that the kiss had not happened. And then she felt disappointment with her disappointment. Who was she turning into? She had kissed one man this evening, poor Thomas. She'd forced herself upon him, and clearly he hadn't been all that interested. And here she was not hours later holding onto another man. Of course she reminded herself she'd been using Thomas to gain Francis's attentions and it seemed to have worked. She thought again of Thomas, and the look in his eyes. She wished she could have taken it back and spared him the discomfort and embarrassment.

They stopped in front of her door and she smiled as she released Francis's arm.

"Goodnight, Betty," he said as he offered her a formal parting bow.

She curtsied in turn. "Goodnight, Mr. Garrett. Thank you for the escort home."

He stared at her for a long moment and she was sure he would swoop in for a kiss, but then his eyes darted to the second story window. He offered her a courteous nod and turned to walk back the way he came, heading towards his home or the tavern. There was no telling what the menfolk actually did between evening and dawn. She squinted up at the window and let out a little sigh at the sight of her father glaring down at her, stealing from her the moment to discover whether her kiss with Thomas had been unusual or significant.

She moved inside and undid her cape as she climbed the stairs. The house was silent and her shadow flickered on the wall from the candle left burning in the hallway. Betty stopped in front of her father's bedroom and put her hand up to the wood. "I am home, Father."

She waited. There was no response.

That suited her just fine for now. She didn't want to discuss her behavior, the dress, or the jewels. She wanted to lie in bed and conspire how she might get Francis Garrett to finally kiss her.

Chapter Six

Betty woke to the sound of her father's shoes shuffling across the worn floorboards of her room. The creak of the jewelry box was like a knife in her heart as he collected her mother's jewels from their place on the top of her trunk. She hadn't had time to respond—she'd barely seen him depart with the box under his arm. Pulling the covers back, she stared longingly at where the jewels had been moments before. Betty could cry, or she could work out a plan to fix the mess she'd gotten herself into. Crying would solve nothing so she got to work. She was still on a mission and time was quickly running out.

Over breakfast, she reread Mary's letter carefully, checking to see if there was anything she'd overlooked. She stuffed it into her pocket when her father came back into the kitchen.

"Church services will be starting soon. Have you eaten?"

He sat down at the table and pulled a bowl of steaming hot cereal towards himself. He did not look at her as he spooned the hot mush into his mouth.

She ate as well, bothered terribly that her father was resorting to such childish behavior. She was an adult and he should have consulted with her before making a decision for the both of them. There was no reason he had to rush away to England now. He could wait until she was married.

"Why must we travel so soon, Father?"

His jaw clenched at her question but he gave no response.

"I do not wish to go back to England. I wish to stay here. If you had given me some warning I could have been courting and found someone to care for me. But now I have no choice."

"You would not be happy here, Betty. Mark my words, there will be nothing short of heartache here soon. I don't want you stuck in the middle of it with no way out."

"I don't belong there. I don't remember England. This is my home. Why can you not understand that?"

He slammed his fist on the table. "I understand that you are a strong-willed girl, Betty. And I understand that you are throwing a tantrum like a small child. It does not matter what you do, short of taking your own life, for which God will banish you to burn in hell. You are leaving with me for England."

"But—"

"Enough." That one word, said so forcefully, was enough to make her shut her mouth. Betty knew where the limit was and she'd already gone well past it.

She cleaned up their dishes and went above stairs to put on her Sunday clothes. Once she was ready, she went downstairs and waited for him to join her.

The church service was uneventful aside from spotting Francis as he walked into his private familial pew. She'd tried to get his attention but he did not turn back to stare up at the general public in the high pews. And why should he? A chill passed over Betty when Francis leaned over and pressed a polite kiss to Grace's cheek, before taking his seat next to her.

That kiss was on Betty's mind the whole of the service, and when it was over she had no idea of what the topic had been about. They were released and met on the street outside to congregate as they normally did Sunday mornings. The church bells rang low and proud as she was stopped by a hand upon her elbow. The prickles that raced along her skin, did not prepare her for finding Thomas standing behind her.

He bowed and she curtsied. "Good day," he said.

She nodded and waited. His face transformed from determination to impatience very quickly.

"I wanted to apologize for my behavior last evening."

She wet her lips quickly and dropped her gaze. "No, I apologize for making a public spectacle of the two of us."

His finger went beneath her chin and lifted it ever so slightly until she was meeting his gaze. Movement out of the corner of her eye drew her attention away for a moment. Francis was coming. With her heart beating rapidly in her chest, she wrapped her arm around Thomas's and stepped in close to him.

He was quicker today, however, than he had been the evening before. He removed his arm from her grasp and placed his hands on her shoulders, keeping proper distance between them. "Betty."

She swallowed hard as her cheeks surged with heat. "My apologies," she said. Francis stepped aside to have a chat with George and a few other gentlemen. His back was to her so there was no need for the show. She met Thomas's gaze and he shook his head.

"I have said my apologies, but please allow me to be clear. Do not force a kiss upon me again. If I wish to kiss you then I shall."

She blinked at the apparent harshness of his statement. "Perhaps I do not wish for you to grace me with your kisses, Mr. Murray. Perhaps I was merely feeling pity for your lack of desire among the female population of Williamsburg."

His eyes scanned her body carefully, methodically, and she drew her scarf closer to her bosom.

"What are you doing? Tis indecent."

"Just wondering if your scales are showing. You seem to be as viscous as a snake."

"What are you implying, sir?"

"That while I offer you a compliment, you throw an insult."

"A compliment? You said you do not wish to kiss me."

"Nay. I said when I wish to kiss you, I will make the first move."

"Why must you make the first move?"

"Because that is how tis done, Betty."

She pressed her lips into a hard line and shook her head. She caught sight of her father in the distance, and narrowed her gaze to try to see better. Thomas turned his head and stared too. "Your father?" he asked.

"Yes."

As they stood observing, her father passed the box containing Betty's mother's jewelry to Mr. Neely, and in exchange his hand was filled with coin.

"Excuse me," Betty said, and the break in her voice gave away her emotional state.

"Betty, wait," Thomas said, following after her. "What was in the box? Something dear to your heart?"

She nodded. "Yes."

"Why is he selling it if it means so much to you? Does he wish to harm you?"

She kept her head down. How did she answer such a question? Did her father wish to harm her? She was no longer sure of the answer. He did not listen to her grievances. He did not buy her new dresses that fit. He was shipping her off to England to become a governess to her cousins. He had not hit her, but but the emotional blow was just as painful. Her heart was being shredded into pieces. The pain of it was pressing against her eyes.

"Betty," he said again, when they were further away from the church. He pulled her aside and in an attempt to hide her face from him and everyone else walking by, she threw herself against his chest. Slowly his arms came around and held her. "Betty," he said again, softer. "You must pull yourself together. We can discuss this but not in the middle of the street. Would you care for a ride?"

She nodded, unable to look at him lest she start crying all over his clothing.

"Come, my carriage is waiting." He pushed her hand into the corner of his arm and led her towards his carriage where his driver was waiting.

She stepped up into it and he joined her. "Why is your father selling things? Is he in financial straits?" Thomas asked when they were safely trotting down the street, the carriage open to the eyes of others so they would not compromise themselves as they rode together.

With nothing but the sound of the horse hooves and the birds singing in the distance, and the feel of the wind blowing on her face, Betty was able to clear her emotions enough to speak. She just needed to keep her eyes on the horses and the road ahead. "He has not been doing well, it's true. The taxes imposed upon him were a great burden. We have lost a great deal of money."

"He is not alone in that. Does he have another trade? Any desire to learn one?"

She shook her head. "Nay." She pressed her lips

together, her fingers fumbling in her lap. Did she dare open up to anyone about her father's plans? "He is moving us back to England." The silence beside her lasted for a long moment and she wasn't sure he'd heard her, but when she looked up, the stitch of Thomas's jaw worked beneath his skin. "Are you alright?"

"When does he plan to move you both to England?"

She swallowed and lied. She wasn't ready to admit to it out loud. "I do not concern myself with the details."

"What was he selling, Betty?"

"My mother's jewelry," she said, turning her face away. Luckily for her it was not uncommon to have dust in your eyes from the street. She dabbed at them gently. "I was hoping to have them when I married."

"Do you wish to be married?"

"Of course."

"For love, or for status?"

"For love. Though a good status would certainly help the marriage to be happier, don't you agree?"

He nodded. "It would make the disagreements of a different nature."

"How so?"

"You may fight over what to spend your earnings on. The blue China pattern versus the pink."

"You must choose the blue. Tis traditional."

He regarded her for a moment and she thought she saw a smile at the corner of his lips—shocking for serious Thomas Murray.

"Did you smile, Mr. Murray?"

"No. I do not smile."

It was her turn to smile. "Just as you do not dance, I suppose?"

"You see what happened when I danced."

"What was that?"

"A madam kissed me. Dancing and smiling make one such as myself irresistible."

"Seems worse things could happen to you, Mr. Murray."

"Very true." He paused and gripped the side of his open carriage as the driver turned them onto a new street. "Tell me how you plan to keep your father from leaving."

She frowned. Could he read her mind?

He cocked an eyebrow at her expression. "Come, Betty. I have known you since we were young. We went to the same school house for a few years. I know you are a schemer. If not by yourself, then at least with the group of ladies you cohort with. What do you have planned?"

She turned her face away from his and huffed loudly.

He chuckled. "I do wish your father the best of luck. Whatever your plans I know he will need it."

"I have no plans. I *had* a plan but it is not going well at all."

"What was it?"

"It doesn't matter. I will have to abandon it because it seems rather unlikely of coming to fruition."

"Fine. Have you given your father ample reason to stay in Williamsburg?"

"Does his daughter's desire mean nothing?"

"Oh I am sure it means a great deal. However, your father is a widower. And he has come upon a rotten round of bad luck. I can tell you there are two things a man needs to be happy and content: money and a madam. He has neither."

She considered that. If what he said was true then perhaps she did have some hope of staying. Francis, while very handsome and well to do, probably would never ask for her hand in marriage. And even if he did ask for her hand, she had no way of knowing how long that could take.

"What do you propose, Mr. Murray?"

"I will not scheme with you, Miss Paca."

"I believe you already have," she said with a grin. "Which should I strive to find first? The money or the madam?"

"The money, of course. You cannot expect a madam to stay without ample money to weigh her down in your pocket."

"Is that so?"

"Sadly it is. That is why I have no madam in my pocket."

"You are incorrect, sir. You have no madam because you find yourself to desire too much control. You should show off your natural talents."

"I suppose you are speaking of dancing?"

She nodded. "And smiling. Show both of those off and you'll have a string of madams wanting to be in your pocket, coin or no."

"Then perhaps your father would be in the same boat. Perhaps he only needs the charms he's been given to woo a woman."

"Perhaps."

After one more trip around the square, Thomas let Betty disembark from the carriage, and he watched her as she crossed the road. The more time spent with Betty Paca, the further she attached herself to his heart. He shook his head, glancing away, but it was no use. She was still firmly in his thoughts. What would it take for him to move on from her? Would he ever have the same feelings for another woman, or were they solely for her?

After she was safely inside her home, he ordered his driver to take him across town to the Purcell's home. He was still determined to figure out what had happened that night and without a name, he was going to have to go digging himself.

It was broad daylight so Thomas made sure he stopped before entering the house to speak with the neighbors. He interviewed the families on either side of the Purcell residence as well as those who resided across the dirt road. No one had heard anything unusual.

"You saw no one unusual coming around in the days before Mr. Purcell's murder?"

"Not that I can recall. What did you say your name was?"

"Mr. Thomas Murray. I am an attorney, and I'm hoping to find something that will help prove the case that Mrs. Purcell did not murder her husband."

The neighbor shook his head slowly. "Tis a shame she will be hanged. He made her life hell, sure as the sun rises, but she loved him. And despite what he did when he was mad with drink he loved her too."

"Alright," Thomas said, disappointed he was no closer to solving the case than he was before. "Thank you for taking the time, Mr. Smallwood. If you recall anything of interest later, please do come call on me at my office or at home."

Mr. Smallwood nodded his acceptance before turning to go back inside.

With no one left to interview, he turned his attention to the house itself. The crude wooden structure was severely leaning and Thomas had no doubt the straw roof leaked gravely whenever a rain came. As he approached, he noted the lock on the front door only *appeared* to be closed. He lifted the lock and held it in his hand as he opened the door and went into the house.

It smelled tremendously and Thomas had to cover his mouth with his cravat to keep from gagging. The chamber pots had been left and no one had bothered to clean up the gore covering the floor near the front door. The smell of rotten blood and human excrement filled the small space.

Once he acclimated himself, Thomas carefully stepped around the house, looking for anything that might give away who had been there the evening of the murder. If it had been a crime of passion, he would have expected the bed sheets to be rumpled, but they appeared neatly tucked under the flat straw mattress.

As Mr. Purcell had been murdered by the front

door, the attacker was in one of two places—either in front of the victim, or behind him. Thomas put his hand out to sit down in one of the chairs and noted it was already away from the table. Not only one chair, but two. He wondered if Mrs. Purcell had been sitting at the table conversing with someone. Perhaps Mr. Purcell walked in and started yelling from the doorway. The murderer grabbed the knife from the table and ran Mr. Purcell through with it.

Thomas shook his head as he stared at the blood stains on the dirt floor. Would he ever know what happened? Clearly Mrs. Purcell was the key and she would not speak a word.

The smells were quickly making him ill. With a cough, Thomas exited the house, careful not to disturb the ghostly scene. He put the lock back on the door and as he turned, he noted several foot-prints in the dirt. The foot prints on the ground leading away from the house, stopped beside some old carriage tracks. It would be hard for one not to notice a carriage stopping in front of these homes.

Thomas lifted his eyes and glanced around. When he'd arrived, everyone had been out of doors, doing their cooking, laundry, and gardening. Now they had disappeared into their homes. Thomas's jaw clenched tightly. They were scared, and there was nothing

Thomas could say to reassure them they would be safe from harm.

Upon closer inspection, Thomas noted there were two sets of footprints that led to the carriage. One of a man, and the other of a woman.

Someone with power committed this crime and none of these folks were going to speak out against him or her, as the foot prints suggested.

He had enough to chew on for now. He would sit with the information and hope something came to him in haste. The trial would be held soon enough, and if he did not have anything by, then Mrs. Purcell would hang.

Chapter Seven

Betty's mind had been aflutter all evening as she busily schemed. Who, she thought, could possibly make Father such a good match he would no longer desire to leave Virginia? What woman did she know who was unmarried and could use his skills as a merchant?

That evening she'd dreamt of the solution. It seemed pondering something long enough would drive God to provide the answer overnight.

She was as cheery as could be when she left the house and headed down Duke of Gloucester towards Madam McDowell's shop. The answer had been in front of her all evening, literally. She'd stared at the dress in the evening light, not knowing why it had shimmered—but she knew now. The dress was her hope. The creator her savior.

She was nearly at the shop when she ran into from someone stepping out the door. Flustered she managed to look up as the gentleman's hands settled on her forearms. Twas Thomas.

"Whatever are you doing here?" Betty asked, her body suddenly breathless, though she blamed that on him pummeling into her. It had nothing to do with the way his lips quirked at the corners, or how he smelled faintly of sandalwood.

"I was merely running an errand for my mother," he confessed. He let her go and took a step back. "What are *you* doing here?" he returned the question, his eyebrows raising suspiciously. "Not purchasing another dress, I hope."

She blushed at the accusation and she shook her head. "No. I..." Her voice dropped from her throat. "I am going to invite Madam McDowell over to dine with my father."

"Oh? Is there courting going on?"

"There may be. I mean, there *will* be. This will be the first of the courting. If she's interested, of course."

"Of course," he said, smiling.

Betty's insides heated as she took in his handsome face, the strong line of his jaw, the kindness and warmth displayed in his eyes. And his lips... they were so...

"Do not let me interfere with your errand," he said, bowing then stepping aside.

The spell was broken and she smiled in return and moved towards the shop door, mentally shaking memories of kissing Thomas from her mind.

Madam McDowell was behind the long wooden counter. She scribbled something fiercely on a piece of parchment. Betty watched as her head tilted back and forth as she wrote, and wondered if she should excuse herself. It was obvious she was penning something personal.

She signed her name with great flourish, then caught sight of Betty and a startled noise came from her. "Miss Paca, you did scare me."

"My apologies," Betty said softly. "You seemed very intent on your writing. I did not wish to disturb you."

"What can I do for you today?" she asked, carefully setting aside her parchment. "Would you care to order another dress for your collection?" Her hand motioned to Betty's outfit, still too tight, still too torn and tattered for a girl of her station.

"No. I have come to discuss something else with you."

"Oh?" She came around the counter and motioned to a pair of soft seats in the middle of the shop. "What would you like to discuss, my dear?"

"My father."

Madam McDowell nodded as she put her hands daintily on her knees and inched forward. "Yes? What about your father?"

Betty wasn't quite sure how to breach this topic of conversation and so she started with, "What do you think of him?"

"Why, I think he is a very respectable man."

"And handsome? Do you think him handsome?"

Betty held her breath as she watched Madam McDowell's eyes roll towards the ceiling as she considered the question. If she did not find her father appealing then Betty would yet again be back to the beginning.

Madam McDowell laughed softly. "I do suppose he is easy on the eyes."

Betty's sigh was audible and it made Madam McDowell laugh once more.

"My father was hoping to have your company for dinner this evening, at our residence."

Her eyes fluttered and a hand went to her chest. Betty's gut tightened. This was it. She steeled herself for the rejection that did not come.

"That sounds like a wonderful offer. What time will your father be serving dinner?"

"Just past dark," Betty said, clasping her hands to her chest. She was so relieved that Madam McDowell had said yes. She was lovely and a widow, and it was clear Betty's father could help her with business endeavors if they decided to court each other. Honestly, she couldn't see why they wouldn't. In her mind's eye she could already see them standing aside the fire, taking each other's hand and saying their promises of marriage. "Nothing too formal, mind you. He is a simple man at heart."

Madam McDowell winked at her, also offered her a simple nod. "Of course."

"Oh and please do not mention the debt he's owed to you unless he asks you first."

There was a flash of shock in her eyes, but it quickly faded. Perhaps she wasn't used to ladies discussing business beneath their father's noses. Betty shrugged it off and waved as she saw herself out of the shop.

One problem was on the way to being solved. Of course she still had the matter of Francis. It was probable this dinner could all go terribly wrong, and she wasn't one to put all her eggs into one basket. Her father had often told her that, especially when the British taxes on molasses came to pass.

She still needed to catch and keep Francis's attention. Dancing with Thomas had seemed to have an effect, perhaps more of Thomas would do the trick, though she didn't notice Francis staring at her after church the previous day when she'd driven off with Thomas. She hadn't been looking either, she'd been too caught up in trying to keep her emotions from showing. Aside from Thomas, what could she do to capture Francis's attention? The only thing she had to go off of were her own feelings. If a man wanted to capture her attention there would be one way for sure that would work: a gift.

She glanced in the window of the general store and paused to admire the variety of goods it held. She nibbled on her lower lip as she assessed every item on display in the window and then looked over her shoulders to see if anyone was staring at her. Of course they were not, they were too busy running their own errands. She went back to her perusal of the shop window and her attention caught on a glittering pocket watch. The silver top sparkled and begged to be engraved. She worried her lip a bit more and then popped into the shop. For if a man were to leave her a gift as extravagant as this one there would be no way she could turn him down.

It took longer than she'd expected for the engraving. Everyone was buying goods this time of day and when she'd arrived at the Silversmith, she'd had to wait until he returned from lunch with his wife.

When he arrived back he took his time getting settled, and with much patience the task was finally completed. Betty admired the watch against her palm. She was sure Francis would love it. How could he not?

She was just stepping onto Duke of Gloucester Street when the sky cracked open with thunder and the rain poured down onto Williamsburg and anyone silly enough to be caught up in the bad weather. Betty was included in that count. She picked up her skirts, which were quickly growing dirty from the muddied street beneath her feet, and covered her head with her hand. She saw the covered porch of the Raleigh Tavern and was almost to it when she was almost to it when the clatter of hooves and the creak of strained wheels came from her right.

When she looked up too late, the horses were coming at her. Shocked, she froze in place. They raced closer. Her life played before her eyes and she clutched the pocket watch close to her chest as she shut her eyes tight. Her breath left her as she was vaulted forward, a pair of hands heavy on her backside as she was tackled out of harm's way. A body behind her, she forcefully collided with a horse post and her breath left her. She sucked in deep breaths, panic causing them to come painfully.

"Shh, Betty, tis alright. You are not harmed." Thomas's soft, reassuring voice tickled her ear. He turned her in his arms and looked her over carefully. "You were almost as flat as the ground beneath us," he said softly, his eyes alight with what appeared to be anger.

With a hand to her chest, she tried very hard to draw breath. It was no use. Her inhales were too shallow, too quick. When Thomas realized her struggle, he pulled her with him into the tavern. In a dark corner where pondering eyes would not be able to see much, he sat her down next to him and with nimble fingers he loosened her stays.

Her gasp was for a different reason now, and she put a hand behind her back to try to tangle the stay strings in her fingers. "Please, sir, we are in public."

"I do not know why you ladies insist on wearing such ridiculous garments. You need to be able to breathe." He shifted in his seat as he removed his coat and perched it onto her shoulders. "Now no one will be the wiser," he said as he combed the rain from his light brown hair. His eyes took in the room and he nodded as the waitress came to take their order. Thomas ordered for the both of them, then sat back once she was gone and they were again alone.

Betty was sitting next to her savior. She would have hated to think what would have become of her if he hadn't come to her rescue.

He frowned at the wide-eyed look on her face. "Why are you staring at me in such a fashion?"

She said nothing.

"Betty?" he asked, leaning forward ever so slightly to get a better look at her face in the dim flickering candlelight. All she could think of was thanking him. But how does one thank a man for saving her life? It felt natural when she leaned forward and pressed her lips to his. Once again he was caught off guard, and after a moment of tasting her, he turned his head and scooted away. He sighed heavily, his shoulders slumped as if he were disappointed. "Why must you insist on doing that?"

"I apologize. I do not know what came over me, perhaps it was the brush with death. I—I am very deeply sorry." She grabbed the lapels of his coat and pulled them closer together. This man did nothing but let her know how very much he disliked kissing her. He'd saved her because he was a gentleman. He'd saved her because he saw a person in danger. She was reading so much more into it than there was. She was a fool.

When his ale arrived he took a long pull from it before setting it down on the table. Patrons were chattering all around them, gay with the company they were keeping. The awkwardness was reserved for their table, it seemed, and she was the cause of it all.

“Thank you for saving me,” she said. “But I should be going. I will let you enjoy your spirits.” She did not get the coat but a few inches off her shoulders before he tugging it back into place.

“Do not be silly, Betty. You will stay. Tis still raining outside and you will catch your death if you go out there. Enjoy your warm cider and tell me of your day.”

She swallowed the lump in her throat as she stared at the cider, still steaming, in front of her. “My day?”

“Yes. I’m sure it was infinitely more interesting than my own. Would you care for me to indulge you first? Fine. I woke, broke my fast, and then went to my office where I met with not one, but two men who inquired about legal documents to disband their marriages. They had just come from the paper where they’d placed their advertisements against their wives. On the one hand, I wish I could grant them the document they require because it would mean a great income to myself, but divorce is still very much illegal, and on the other, I do not feel one bit sorry for them. It is well known how they treated their wives, and why their wives both decided to leave. If anyone should have sought my legal counsel it should have been the female parties."

Betty knew the parties of whom he spoke, in the small town of Williamsburg it was hard not to know your neighbors. Clara Deane and Tilly Mercer, a few years senior to Betty, had been seen around town a fortnight prior purchasing unusual provisions on their husband's credit. She heard many stories and they all seemed to point to the same conclusion, since between them they'd only purchased one trunk. And she'd seen the two women secretly embrace each other. "Mistreatment aside, it was my understanding they left... together?" she asked, furrowing her brow as she sipped her cider to keep her mouth from saying more.

Thomas nearly spit out the ale he was partaking and when he glanced at her, he chuckled. "I thought that was but some sick drunkard's fantasy, or idle gossip?"

She shrugged her slender shoulders. "I could not say, except that I saw them kissing once behind John Greenhow's store. I was quite shocked, and it took me a few days to convince myself that I must have been seeing things, but after they left the city together... there was no mistaking what I'd seen."

He stared at her for a beat too long and shook his head. "I did not take you for a gossip, Betty Paca."

"I am not a gossip, sir. Had I been a gossip I would have told someone what I had seen. As it were you are the first who I have told." The realization struck Betty at the same moment she made the declaration. Why had she chosen to confide in him? What was it about Thomas that put her so at ease, yet at the same time sent her body fluttering?

He smiled at her admission. Whether it was to her not being a gossip or to her only sharing her secrets with him, she could not tell. She shifted in her seat under his scrutiny. "Why do you stare at me so?" she asked.

He glanced away towards his cup of ale. "Do you not know already?"

Her mind danced over the reasons. Was she dirty from the rain? Was her hair out of place? She glanced down and examined her chest, but no, everything was as decent as could be expected with her loosened stays. She looked back to him and shook her head. "Nay, I do not know."

He looked up to her and she felt her insides melting, the heat of it rising to her cheeks. His eyes sparkled in the dancing candlelight. "You are quite a beauty, Miss Paca."

Her body knew what he was admitting before her brain did. "Thank you," she said softly as she looked away.

He cleared his throat and sat up in his seat. "I have embarrassed you. Of course you would be embarrassed. I'm not nearly as handsome as the man you really wish to compliment you."

"No, tis not that," she said, reaching for his arm. His eyes dropped to her fingers and that now familiar heat flooded her stomach. She quickly removed her hand and pulled the coat back around her again, as if it would offer her protection.

"What is it then?"

"Gentlemen have not paid me compliments before. Tis new to me."

He chuckled again and shook his head as he took a pull from his cup. "That I do not believe."

She smirked just a little. It was so nice to be the reason for someone else's laughter. "Believe it."

"I cannot. I refuse," he said, turning towards her once again. Her breath seemed to leave her body as he came closer. Her eyes dropped to his lips and it stilled him. "The rain will not let up any time soon. Are you hungry?"

"Famished," she replied softly.

Chapter Eight

When they had filled their bellies and the rain had ceased, Thomas and Betty took to the streets. She glanced at the sky and realized too late that dark had fallen while they'd been inside talking, eating, and enjoying each other's company. A player had performed inside and she'd thoroughly enjoyed joining in with the singing. And she'd even had another dance with Thomas when another gentleman came over and offered to take her for a whirl.

She groaned now, seeing the sky, and Thomas looked at her with confusion. "Is everything alright?"

She shook her head. "No, nothing tis right today. I should have had dinner waiting on the table and given my father instructions on how to dress."

"Dress?"

She turned to Thomas, a bit of guilt on her brow. "I asked Madam McDowell to dine with him."

Thomas nodded. "Yes, and?"

Betty stared up at him and his expression slowly changed from one of confusion, to understanding, and then pity.

"He does not know."

She shook her head. "And neither does she. She assumes he will be expecting her. I would almost rather not return home," she said gloomily.

"Take a longer walk with me instead," he said.

"Walk with you? Our shoes are nearly wet through."

"I find it a small price to pay for more of your company."

A blush once again heated her cheeks. "Where will we walk? Around town? Others will think you are courting me."

"And that would be a terrible mistake?"

She paused. If Francis saw them together, it could be a push in the right direction for her. Perhaps he would be so overcome with jealousy he'd make a move more quickly because of it. She looked up at Thomas. Did he truly have feelings for her? "Are you attempting to court me, Mr. Murray?"

"I would rather keep you guessing," he said as he offered her his arm.

"I would rather you did not," she said, taking his arm as they started to walk down the streets.

"I know you would not. But tis more fun this way."

"For you, perhaps."

He chuckled.

As they walked the streets with only the dim lamp light to light their way, Thomas felt a warmth growing in his chest. He had tried to deny it but when he was near Betty, it was hard to do. He was fond of her. Beyond that, he did not think he would be able to go on much longer without asking her for courtship. It had weighed on him heavily since she'd divulged the information she would be moving to England. He did not know how much time he had left.

Part of him did not want to act for though the famous playwright would say tis better than to love and lost than to never have loved at all, he was sure he could disagree. For if he let himself care for Betty and become acquainted with her, he was sure he would be ruined for any other woman. She was the one he desired despite her scheming and short temper. She was strong willed, and full of life.

"Betty?"

He had been prepared to say the words, to ask her if she would desire to court him, but as she turned her eyes to him, the words lodged in his throat.

"Yes?"

He looked away and coughed loudly. He was brave in so many things and yet he was such a coward when it came to opening up to this woman. He would not lie to her, it was true, but he would not ask her what he had originally meant to.

"Have you heard any gossip about the Purcells?"

"The wife who murdered her husband?"

He nodded, swallowing back the self depreciation he felt at that moment.

She shrugged. "I was in Mr. Prentis's shop and overheard a couple of younger women speaking about a gentry couple being there."

His ears perked up, he had no idea he would have actually been able to extract information from her. "Did you hear who they thought the gentry might be?"

Betty shook her head. "Nay. When Francis Garrett walked in they stopped speaking and left the store. I did not have a chance to hear."

Thomas's gut coiled. "Did they see his face before they stopped talking?"

Betty frowned. "I do not recall, Thomas, I was not looking at them. Tis rude to stare."

He nodded. "Yes, yes, of course." He sighed heavily and stuffed his hands into the pockets of his breeches.

"What is the matter? Why such interest in the Purcell murder?"

When he glanced at her, he realized she had been studying his face. Oh, she was beautiful in the dim lamp light. His eyes dropped to her lips and he wished for once he didn't have such a high moral code. He wished he could be as free with women as his peers. But he respected her too much to kiss her outside of a courtship. He forced himself to look her in the eye.

"I am hoping to defend Mrs. Purcell. I do not believe she killed her husband."

Betty's eyes widened for a moment before she turned them away.

"Hm. So if Mrs. Purcell did not murder her husband, then who did? What reason would someone have to murder Mr. Purcell? He had no wealth to his name. No title. No land."

"All of this is true. But there must be some reason. Murder does not happen for no reason."

"Perhaps it was a drunken misunderstanding?"

He nodded, though he doubted it. He didn't want

Betty involved, in case he uncovered something dangerous. "Perhaps it was," he said and then smiled as he attempted to change their topic of conversation. "We should probably stop soon and fix your stays, Miss Paca."

Betty blushed and dropped her eyes as her hands went flat against the middle of her dress. "Yes, Mr. Murray, that would be wise."

"Come, over here." He led her into a darkened corner. Once they were hidden, he stepped behind her and removed his coat from her shoulders. He slid it onto his frame as fast as he could so she would not be indecent for long. If someone happened to come walking past, they would both be in a very precarious situation.

He felt her shudder as he put his hands on the laces at the back of her stays. With gentle tugs, he slowly closed them up.

"Tighter, please, Mr. Murray," Betty insisted. She winced when he pulled them tighter.

"I do not understand," he muttered as he loosened the ties once more. Once she was secure, he moved around to the front of her and offered her his coat again for the air still had a bit of chill to it, and her clothes were still damp.

After slipping into his coat, she turned her chin up and smiled at him, causing his heart to hammer in his chest. "Mr. Murray, you are rather good at tying up a dress. Have you had experience with it before?"

Thomas muttered as his cheeks burned. She was chuckling softly as they walked arm in arm down the road once more.

"Whether I have or have not is no business of yours, Miss Paca, but if it were, which answer would you prefer?"

"The truth," she said.

Chapter Nine

It was late when they arrived back to Betty's home. The house was dark, and she prayed her father had turned in early.

She turned to Thomas, handed him his coat, and curtsied. With her goodbye, she wondered which of two things would happen. Would he kiss her? Or would he let her walk away? Her heart was beating wildly in her chest with anticipation. "Good evening, Mr. Murray. Thank you for the stroll."

He bowed. "Good evening, Miss Paca."

He made no further move to lean in. Her heart sank in her chest. She felt foolish for even thinking he would. It was obvious he was just teasing her, walking with her for companionship and to jest with her. Perhaps he was lonely. Perhaps he was not unlike the two wives who had run away together and his lust was not for the opposite gender.

With a small smile, she nodded her goodbye and went inside.

It was mostly dark, but the fire in the hearth crackled softly.

"Where have you been?"

Betty jumped at the sound of her father's voice. She had not seen him sitting at the table. He had the slump of a man who'd imbibed too hard.

"I was walking with Thomas Murray, Father. I was caught in the rain and had dinner at the Raleigh Tavern."

"Dinner at the Raleigh Tavern? That sounds pleasant. And did Mr. Murray offer up coin for it?"

She swallowed hard and stuck her hand into her pocket. They were back to money again. "He did." But he had not purchased the silver pocket watch she now clutched in her pocket.

"Do you know who paid me a visit this evening?" he asked, his words slightly slurred. He studied her face and did not give her time to respond. "Ah, you do. *You* set it up. A dinner with the widow Madam McDowell." He held a knife in his left hand and was slowly scraping it along the surface of the table. "I need you to know, Betty, that no matter how many tricks you try in the days coming, it will not change the outcome of what is to be."

A large lump formed in her throat, sinking into her chest. She had not known she could fall lower than when Thomas refused to kiss her. But she had. Her plan had not worked and she was doomed to sail off to England. "I thought perhaps you were lonely, Father."

He scoffed. "You did not think of me. You were only thinking of yourself. You have become quite the rebel as of late."

"Father, I—"

He held up his hand and chuckled. "Betty. You remind me so much of your mother. Twas her dream to come to the colonies, not mine. I did as she asked because I loved her. And I love you, Betty, do not mistake my words. And you are right, I am lonely. I am lonely for my country. I miss England. I miss the rolling hills and the smells of the countryside. You do not remember it, but you will learn to love it all the same, Betty."

You will learn to love it all the same.

How could she love it all the same? She knew not one soul across the sea. She would be leaving her friends and everything familiar to her. She would be starting over in a lower station than she even was right now. Her prospects for a good marriage were much improved here in the colonies. The trip back alone could very well be the death of her. And if that were not enough, all her memories of her mother were here. Leaving the colonies made Betty feel like she was leaving her mother behind forever.

Tears pricked at her eyes. Her father was opening up to her and she was in part the cause of his pain. "Then you will understand why I do not want to leave my home either, Father. This place is all I've ever known."

He shook his head and sighed heavily. "Betty, if you wish to come back, you can find a husband and make him sail you across the ocean as your mother had me do her. Please do not cause your father further trouble. I am only doing as I see best."

Panic was fluttering in her chest, a glimmer of hope shining through. Perhaps if she made him see another, better way, he would stay. "You could become rich with widow Madam McDowell. She is in need of a supplier, Father. She's in need of someone to help her manager her affairs better. She told me herself."

He stood up from the table and shook his head. "But I do not wish to help her. I wish to return to my home." He walked over to her and pressed a kiss to her head. "Good night, Betty."

She watched him go above stairs and when he

disappeared from her sight, the tears finally spilled. She ran above stairs and threw herself onto her bed. It was much later, when she'd finally worn herself out, that she decided she couldn't give up yet. She could still catch a husband.

Chapter Ten

Early the next morning Betty was walking out the door when her father came down. “Where are you going?” he asked as she donned her cape.

“I am going to seek some extra work, Father. I feel very badly about the dress. I wish to make sure I pay you back for it with my own labor.”

His gaze dropped and a guilty look crossed his face. “No need for that, Betty. It was overdue.”

“No matter. I am still going to find something to keep myself busy. I do not want you thinking I’m plotting behind your back while you are trying to settle the last of your affairs.”

His jaw was set tight and for a moment, he paused. “Your actions of late do not speak to your ability to keep your word. Scheming will be a waste of your last days in the colonies, Betty. Spend your day wisely. Say your goodbyes to your friends. Laugh your last laughs with them. Memorize their mannerisms. You will soon miss them." He turned away, dismissing her.

She did not heed her father's words as she stepped outside and headed towards Palace Green Street. She had to deliver the gift to Francis before he departed for the day, as she wanted to be sure he would think of no one but her for the remainder of it.

She stood at the bottom of his stairs and stared up at the stately house. Through the window, his family's servants moved about. If she returned to the colonies on her own, it was likely she would come back as one of the servants—the middling class. She would work her way out of debt and perhaps find herself a husband to marry. It may be worth it to stay here in the colonies than to go back overseas.

The front door opened and the lady of the house stepped out onto the stairs. She raised her brows at Betty. "Good morning. Do you have business here this morning?" She regarded the paper wrapped package in Betty's hands.

"Y-yes," she stammered as she held it to her chest. "I have come to deliver something to Francis Garrett. Is he home?"

"He is breaking his fast." She stepped down to

meet Betty and held out her hand for the package. "I will be sure he receives it."

Betty stared down at the package and wished she'd taken the time to scribe something on the brown paper. "Could I not deliver it myself?"

Mrs. Garrett shook her head. "I am afraid not."

Betty reluctantly handed the package over. "Tis from Betty. Please let him know."

She nodded and turned on her heel, heading back into the house. Betty stared at the closed door for a long moment before turning and headed towards the shoemaker's shop. She'd done cuttings for him before, perhaps he was running behind again and could use her help.

She'd first stopped by the storekeeper who had taken the jewels from her father and begged him to set them aside for a fortnight. If her extra work paid off, there was a slight chance she could purchase her mother's jewels back.

The first step to that plan was to acquire work. Luckily, the shoemaker had plenty of pieces that needed to be cut. After returning home, she immediately begun the work. It kept her busy all afternoon and well into the beginning part of the evening, when she had to stop and see to preparing food for dinner.

After putting the cuttings aside in a basket by hearth, she stared out the window for the first time in hours and let out a sigh. She tried to memorize it all, the sounds, the sights, the feelings it stirred in her. She did not know how many more days she would be lucky enough to experience it.

A short while later, a knock came to the door as she was preparing the bread for the fire. She hurried over and opened it, surprised to see Thomas standing there.

"Mr. Murray."

He bowed and she quickly curtsied. "Miss Paca."

When she continued to stand there and stare, he raised his eyebrows. "May I come in?"

"Oh, yes," she stepped back and let him in, suddenly self conscious about the lack of nice furnishings. Thomas Murray was not of her class, he was gentry, and Betty was more than certain the size of her accommodations would fit into his parent's ballroom.

He did not seem to stare nor his eyes linger about as he stepped inside and turned to her. "I have brought you something."

She had not expected this. Her eyes wandered over his body, taking in the way his muscles bunched and released beneath his coat. She had been expecting a lovely pin or a piece of jewelry. What she hadn't expected was the little fluffy ball of dirty matted fur between his large hands.

She furrowed her brows and moved her head to one side and then the other to get a good look at it.

"Tis a kitten. I found it digging through some rubbish behind the tavern."

Her eyes raised to his when he mentioned being behind the tavern. It was well known what happened back there, away from prying eyes. To her surprise, he actually blushed.

"Twas not—"

"You need not lie, Mr. Murray."

"I would never lie to you, Miss Paca. I was behind the tavern because I thought I saw someone I knew."

She perched an inquisitive brow and he opened his mouth to say more, but then the kitten let out a loud mewl. Betty put her hands to her chest, sure it would burst. The little creature was so pitiful looking amongst Thomas's fine clothing, Betty grabbed her up and held her close to her chest. She'd always wanted a pet, but her father said they could not keep one. They did not have time to care for it, and loving an animal that lived on the street was only asking for pain. She made a mistake in holding the tiny beast, for once she felt the soothing purr against her heart she knew she would not bare to be apart from it.

Betty looked up at Thomas who was staring at her with patience. "Thank you, Mr. Murray."

He nodded and clasped his hands behind his back. He rocked on his heels. "What will you name it?"

Betty pet the little creature with the pad of her finger, it's little head forced back slightly with every stroke. "I think Raleigh would be fitting."

"Twould be, had it been found behind the Raleigh tavern. I found it behind the Blue Bell Tavern."

It was her turn to flush. Those seeding dealings did not happen behind the Blue Bell tavern. "Then I shall call it Blue Bell. It is decided."

He gave another nod. She met his eyes when he said no more and caught him staring at her. "Did you wish for me to give you a kiss as a show of my gratefulness, Mr. Murray?"

He grunted and shook his head. "No, Miss Paca. You should not kiss men. We have been over this too many times to count. I need to be going. Good day." He glanced back just once, before leaving her alone with her new companion.

Betty smiled at Blue Bell after Thomas left. "I do not believe him fully, do you?" Teasing Thomas had perhaps not been the most kind thing to do, but she did enjoy it all the same. And she had only been half teasing, for if he had admitted to wanting a kiss she would have happily obliged. Remembering their first embrace, a flash of heat lit up her cheeks. Perhaps soon she would know if Francis's kiss would live up to Thomas's, which seemed to be burned into her memory.

Turning her attention to the fluffy creature in her arms, she flipped the kitten onto its back and after a quick examination righted it again. "*Mr*. Blue Bell. At least we will not have to worry about any more kittens. Let us get you cleaned up. I'm sure you're hungry. You can lie by the fire while I finished preparing supper."

Her evening meal preparation had been more pleasant than usual. The kitten, who turned out not to be as gray and brown as he'd appeared, but was now almost pure white, with stripes of brown upon his back, was fond of chasing her apron strings. And he loved to climb. She nearly howled twice when he decided to use her as a tree trunk. Her father was late, but she had barely had the inclination to notice. With Mr. Blue Bell to keep her company, she was not lonely.

What she lacked in loneliness, she made up for in fatigue. Once the meal was made, she went above stairs to wait for her father. She laid back on her bed, and with the little kitten curled against her midriff, she fell asleep.

It was still dark when she woke again. The kitten was no longer by her side but was chasing the moths that fluttered towards the lamplight in the corner. Betty got up and carefully grabbed up the kitten. He needed to go outside to do his business and she needed to eat something. She crept by her father's bedroom. The door was closed, which must have meant he'd come home.

She set the cat into the grass behind their home and stared at the evening sky. She hated to be out of doors at this hour of the night, it seemed the darkness was charged with eerie ethereal things. She always felt as if she were being watched, and not in a good way. After the kitten had scratched in the dirt she brought him back inside and sat down to eat.

Chapter Eleven

"Betty?"

Betty paused aside the apothecary when she heard her name called. Turning, she smiled as Mary approached, her female servant behind her, hands full of envelopes. Mary spoke something to her servant and after a nod she continued on walking.

"Good day, Betty Paca."

Betty nodded. "Good day, Mrs. Bordley. Married life suits you very well."

Mary laughed and pretended to preen her hair. "It does, does it not? How is your quest to join the class of married women?"

It had been a few days since she'd delivered the pocket watch to Francis's house, and she hadn't heard anything from him. She suspected he was beyond flattered and unsure of what move to make next. But there was a slight niggling in her head that warned her against being so sure of herself. Should she confide in Mary? If you could not confide in your friend, who could you confide in at all?

Betty took a step closer and gently entwined her arm with Mary's, getting closer so they would not be overheard. "I'm not altogether sure, Mary."

Mary's face tilted slightly, a worried frown on her forehead. "How do you mean?"

"I'm still trying to gain Francis's attentions."

Mary eyebrows rose in surprise. "Francis? I'd heard you have been wandering around the streets of Williamsburg with Thomas Murray."

Thomas Murray. Was *he* the reason why Francis had not come calling on her? Had she made a grave mistake? "I have, but that was only so Francis might start to notice I am currently courting."

Mary considered this for a moment and nodded. "I see. In that case, you should go ahead and move on to the next step in the letter, my dear Betty. I have just sent my servant to deliver invitations. My mother-in-law is throwing a ball on short notice to celebrate the lift in the sugar taxes. I do hope you'll be able to attend. It will be another chance for you to dance with your beloved Francis." She smiled sweetly, pressed a soft kiss to Betty's cheek, and took a step back.

Another ball? Twas turning out to be a busy season, and officially the season had yet to start. She would not complain, however. The more dances she attended, the better chance she had at finding a husband and staying in the colonies. "I would not miss it for all the stars in the sky," Betty replied.

Mary grinned. "That is wonderful news. Take care, Betty. I will see you soon."

Betty delivered more parts to the shoemaker and stuffed the coin she received into her pocket. She finally had enough to pay off the debt she owed to Mr. Prentis, but she was still working off the debt she owed to her father for her mother's jewelry. She had gone the day after she'd seen her father selling it to beg the storekeeper to set it aside for her. He'd reluctantly agreed. She wasn't sure she would be able to acquire the funds necessary, but she at least had to try.

After collecting her next batch of leathers she paid off her debt with Mr. Prentis. She was almost out of the door when she overheard Francis's voice. She paused by the exit and pretended to be looking at the display near the window.

"Thank you for the compliments, Mr. Prentis.

Twas a gift from my mother. I came to ask if you could please change the engraving on it. I wish to gift it to my protégé. We have very similar initials. You could change the F into a B and add an S, could you not?"

Mr. Prentis's eyes turned to Betty. She saw his reflection in the glass and quickly left the store. Francis did not even know the watch was from her. Her plan had been foiled by his mother. And the woman was sitting in the carriage outside the store.

Betty was tired of being pushed around by her elders. She was a woman now too, and it was time she took charge. She was not of the gentry class like Mrs. Garrett, but she was not a child or a horse who she could whip into submission either. Betty considered leaving but her feet had other plans, and she approached the carriage.

"Mrs. Garrett, might I speak with you for a moment?"

Mrs. Garrett looked down at her and smirked. "My dear, I have no business with the likes of you."

"You promised me you would deliver the package to Francis."

"And I did."

"I just overheard him telling Mr. Prentis it twas a gift from his mother. Twas not a gift from you. Twas a gift from me."

She shrugged a shoulder and refused to meet her eyes. "He would not have known who it was from anyway, dear. He is spoken for. He will marry in his class and that is the end of it. I've saved you heartache and time, my dear. You should be thanking me."

Betty had never felt as low or inferior as she did in that moment. This woman had been born in England and had come over with her parents. She came from money and she thought those without were lesser. Betty knew she was no lesser than any other person alive. They were all people. They all deserved kindness and decency.

People like Mrs. Garrett made her angry. Without thinking about the consequences, Betty stooped down, grabbed a handful of mud, and flung it at the carriage. She gasped when her actions caught up with her brain, and blinked at the stunned image of Mrs. Garrett, the right side of her face covered in a mixture of mud, horse droppings, and urine. She started sputtering and the carriage driver climbed down from his seat.

Betty picked up her skirts and ran as quickly as she could from the incident. When she was far enough away, she looked over her shoulder and saw Francis's head turn in her direction. He started running after her. She turned back around and ran as fast as her stays would allow her. Once she started to feel light headed, she quickly stepped into the closest public space. She shut the door behind her, leaned on it with all of her dainty weight, and struggled to catch her breath.

"Betty?"

Upon opening her eyes, Betty took in the small dark oak panelled walls and large reclining black leather chair of the barber's shop. Reclined in the chair was Mr. Murray and Mr. Murray was in half a state of dress, his chest bare so as not to ruin his coat and shirt. Her breath still had not returned enough to speak. She closed her eyes and shook her head, holding up one dirty hand as she covered her eyes with the clean one.

She reached out and found a seat just as the door was flung open again. Her eyes widened as she stared into the angry eyes of Francis Garrett.

"You? *You* threw excrement at my mother! Explain yourself!"

Betty heard Thomas and the barber chuckling softly. She did not think it very funny at all.

"I was aiming for the carriage," she said. "Twas not her luck that my aim is terrible."

The chuckles changed to laughter and Francis's face turned even redder. "You owe her an apology."

"I'm sorry, sir, but I am owed an apology first."

"What for? What has she done to you besides look the other way when you cross her path?"

Betty swallowed down her shame. She had no idea Francis was as elitist as his mother. Perhaps the apple did not fall so far from the tree. "Nothing, sir. I was mistaken. I will give her a proper apology within a fortnight."

He stood there, his fists clenched tightly at his sides. Seeing him this way, hinted at a more brutal side to him, one he would gladly unleash on others. Thomas cleared his throat, letting Francis know he was still present. Francis nodded his acceptance of her terms and left the shop.

Thomas let out a sigh and laid back down to let the barber finish his shave. The barber hummed softly as he made quick with the razor.

Betty stood to leave but heard Thomas's disapproving tone in his throat.

"I believe he wishes you to stay, miss. I shall be finished in a moment."

Betty sat down and waited, staring at the leathers in her lap. She had quite a few less than when she'd left the shop. She knew without even going back to check that a few would be missing. She would not be receiving any money from this batch, she would have to work for a few more days just to make up for the loss she'd now given to the shoe maker. She had no hope of repaying her debts before leaving the colonies with shoe leathers alone. She was going to have to find other ways to supplement.

Betty sighed heavily as she stared at her dirty hand. Her father was right, she was a rebel. She didn't know where it was coming from, it was just happening to her. Like a butterfly emerging from its cocoon. She could not seem to control her actions as of late. She was rather impulsive. Reckless.

She thought, suddenly, of Mrs. Garrett's face. Betty hid her face in the crook of her arm and started to laugh. She couldn't hold it in. The expression of horror and shock would forever be burned into her memory.

So lost in her mirth, she did not hear the rustle of clothes or the footsteps approaching her.

"You are nothing but trouble, Miss Paca," Thomas said as he smiled down at her.

Chapter Twelve

"What did she do?" Thomas inquired as they walked together down the road. Thomas had promised to protect her lest Mrs. Garrett's carriage came driving by.

"I would rather not discuss it."

"No, I'm sure you wouldn't. Whatever it was she said must have hurt you deeply. I remember only once when you acted out in a similar manner."

She frowned and met his gaze. "How do you mean?"

He stared up at the clouded sky, his voice undemanding and soothing as if trying to soften the blow. "Your mother had just died of the pox and you took scissors to Mary's hair. I was surprised the two of you became friends at all after that."

The memory came back. "She said that God only

did what was best. And I was so upset that she implied God taking my mother from me could possibly be good or best."

"She was insensitive, tis true, but she was a child."

Betty nodded. "As was I."

"Yes. I regret that you did not return to school after that."

Betty regretted it too. She'd loved school. She loved reading and math and most of all, she loved feeling as if she belonged somewhere. When she returned home she studied when she could but her father made sure she took the place of her mother's hands with the help of their neighbor. Her lesson that year was in running a household.

She looked up and smiled. "We deal with life as it comes, we have no other choice."

"Life has dealt you a hard hand," he said, turning his eyes away, breaking the little spark of a spell that lay between them.

She did not know how to respond to that. It was true, but there were others whose lives were much harder than her own. She still felt blessed by God. When they reached the front of her house they stopped and she smiled once more. "Always such a gentleman."

"As my mother taught me to be."

She held the leathers tighter against her chest. "I

suppose I should go in and get started. I will have to beg Mr. Wiley for extra work so that I can pay for the leathers I lost."

Thomas regarded her carefully, his eyes roaming her face. Betty could tell he was wrestling something in his mind. "Perhaps you should pay my mother a visit. She is behind on sewing. I am sure she would be more than happy to help if you explain what has happened."

Betty blushed. She wasn't so sure that if Madam Murray knew she'd purchased an extravagant dress without her father's permission, she would be as understanding as Thomas claimed. But it was an opportunity to make extra money, and sewing for a madam would be much more profitable than cutting for Mr. Wiley. And money was something she sorely needed. She nodded. "Thank you, Mr. Murray. I shall pay her a visit."

He nodded in return. The Adam's apple in his throat bobbed curiously several times. He cleared his throat, then took hold of his cap and gave it a tilt. "Good day, Miss Paca."

"Thomas..." She was unsure why she had the urge to confide in him.

He lowered his hand from his hat and raised brows over curious golden eyes. "Yes, Miss Paca?"

"I gave Mrs. Garrett a silver watch to give to

Francis, and I overhead him in Mr. Prentis's shop, claiming it was from his mother and asking to have the engraving changed." Betty felt her cheeks blossom with color and she dropped her gaze to her muddied boots. "You must think me silly," she said softly.

"Silly is not a word I would ever use to describe you, Betty. He does not deserve you."

She dared a glance at his face and her breath caught in her stays. He was staring at her as if he were looking upon a work of Charles Wilson Peale, Williamsburg's finest portrait artist.

He blinked and his eyes clouded over, "I should take my leave. Good day, Betty Paca."

"Good day," she said, watching him turn on his heel and walk away down the dusty and muddied streets. She giggled a little when he turned back and she caught him. Now she knew what kind of man Francis really was, she was beginning to see Thomas differently as well.

Thomas had been nothing but kind. The only thing missing was Thomas's desire for her. She was unsure what to do and could not discuss it with her father. She turned on her heel and headed up the street a little way so she could pay a visit to her friend. Surely Sally could lend some advice over tea.

"You have kissed him and he rebuffed you?"

Betty nodded as she cut on Sally's kitchen table, her mother was outside tending their small garden, leaving the two of them alone to discuss private things.

"That does not bode well, Betty. Perhaps there is another man you'd like to set your sights on?"

Betty sighed softly. "They are all just fine. But I felt the same of Thomas before he touched me."

Sally's bright emerald eyes suddenly came to life as an idea sparked in her head. "Perhaps you would feel more for a man if he touched you? The ball. Your objective there should be to dance with as many suitors as you possibly can. I can help you with that."

Betty chuckled. "That is true. You do dance quite a lot."

"Tis the only way I can eat many little cakes and maintain my slim figure," Sally said, leaning in to whisper as if it were her life's secret.

Betty laughed again. "So teach me, Sally. How does one get so many men to ask her to dance?"

"Well," she took a sip of her tea as she sat perched on the edge of her seat, purposely drawing out the tension. "It's rather easy. You grab a friend and slowly walk in front of a group of men. Then you pause and say, 'Oh, but I wish to dance. I am not seeking a suitor, I just wish to feel the breeze on my cheek, and a gentleman's warm touch upon my back.' And then you walk to the other side of the room, and you smile and look at the gentlemen on the far side of the room. Once one makes eye contact with you, hold it for as long as it takes to count to five and then you look away, sideways. I shall demonstrate." Sally met Betty's gaze and then turned her face to the side, letting her eyes follow, while her shiny brown curls bounced softly against her shoulder. It was a very demure, very innocent gesture.

Betty's dark eyebrows raised with skepticism. "And that always works?"

Sally's innocence quickly faded and Betty's overly cheery smiling friend was back again. "Yes, my dear Betty, without fail. When you leave the ball your feet will be so sore you will wish a duke would come on a white horse and take you home."

"I do not need sore feet to desire that wish," she said.

Sally laughed so hard she bubbled in her tea. Her mother came in from out of doors and gave them both a peculiar look.

Thomas kept his head bent as he cantered down the street, heading towards the edge of town. A note had been sent to him earlier in the morning and he had been summoned back to the Purcell's home. Thomas was utterly excited to be getting somewhere on the case. Aside from the shoe prints and the carriage tracks, he had absolutely nothing.

When he arrived at Mr. Smallwood's home, he found the man outside waiting for him. He nodded to Thomas and led him inside his home. After he'd cleared the threshold, the door was shut firmly behind him.

Thomas stared at the door and the questions on his face must have been obvious for Mr. Smallwood said, "I do not want anyone else seeing you. Thank you, sir, for coming by foot."

Thomas nodded, but was worried he'd made a mistake in coming and not telling anyone where he was going or how long he expected to be gone. "What did you wish to say about the murder, Mr. Smallwood?"

The man laughed nervously and sat down at his small table. "You do not waste time with courteous talk, do you, Mr. Murray?"

"Mrs. Purcell will be hanged if I do not get to

what actually occurred the night her husband was murdered, so in this instance, I do not have much time for pleasantries. I shall ask again, what did you wish to tell about the murder?"

Mr. Smallwood looked down at the center of his table as Thomas stood near the door. Mr. Smallwood's shoulders rose and fell like a man with the weight of a thousand pounds of tobacco sitting upon them. "I was not honest before, sir. I did hear something. I think we all did for when the carriage rode away and we could no longer hear it, we all went running to the Purcell house. The blood..." His voice quieted as his mind took him back and he replayed the memory of stumbling upon the scene in his mind. "I did not know a man would bleed so much when he was punctured."

"Where was he hit, Mr. Smallwood?"

Mr. Smallwood was quiet for a long moment before he lifted his head. "On the back of his head. Mrs. Purcell was screaming something terrible. Her dress was covered with Mr. Purcell's blood. Her hands, her face--all covered with his blood."

"Did you hear any names? Did she utter any names while she was hysterical?"

Mr. Smallwood took a moment before he shook his head. "No. I do not recall her speaking any names, Mr. Murray. But she did say it was all her fault. And she was still saying that when the sheriff came by."

"But it was not Mrs. Purcell who struck Mr. Purcell?"

Mr. Smallwood shook his head sadly. "No, sir. Mrs. Purcell was screaming for them to stop."

"You said 'them', there was more than one assailant?"

Mr. Smallwood swallowed audibly and nodded. "Yes, sir. I could hear two voices outside under Mrs. Purcell's screams. A man and a woman."

"But you did not see anything?"

Mr. Smallwood shook his head. "No, sir. I know this isn't much to go on, but I do hope tis enough to free Mrs. Purcell from gaol."

"Have you received any threats from members of the gentry, Mr. Smallwood?"

"Only one," he said, his eyes narrowed with distrust as he recalled the man's face. "Mr. Paca. Dirty rat bastard cut me out of my share of unloading his ship. He said I stuffed a half dozen silk stockings into my coat. What would a bachelor like myself need with half a dozen silk stockings? That's what I told him, but he didn't pay me no ways. I tried to bring it to court but he threatened me about that too."

"Do you think that Mr. Paca is responsible for this too?"

"It wouldn't surprise me if he were. I know for a fact he has a pretty daughter, maybe it was the two of them come to beat Mr. Purcell for something he didn't do neither."

Thomas nodded as he took in the information. It still made no sense to him that Mr. Paca would attack Mr. Purcell, but Betty said he was lonely and in need of some comfort. Perhaps Thomas was wrong in his assumption and it *had* been a crime of passion. Could it be possible that Mr. Paca was with Mrs. Purcell, and Mr. Purcell came in and caught the two of them in a telling embrace? And while Mr. Purcell was standing in the doorway, Betty came up from behind with a knife and drove it into the back of his head. He shuddered at the thought and shook it away. He could see Betty doing no such thing. And there was one small hole in Smallwood's story—the Paca's did not own a carriage, nor were they considered gentry.

Thomas took in Mr. Smallwood's residence carefully. The fire in the corner was freshly lit. Mr. Smallwood had been elsewhere for most of the day, as the inside of his home still chilled. His eyes drifted to the tiny bed in the corner and Mr. Smallwood's fingers drummed loudly on the table. "Did you need anything else, Mr. Murray?"

Thomas let his gaze flick back to Smallwood. Clearly he was becoming agitated for some reason.

On a hunch, Thomas stepped towards the rumpled bed coverings. "Perhaps. Tell me, do you have straw or feathers in your mattress?"

"Straw or feathers? What does that have to do with the Purcell murder?"

Thomas paused a foot or so away from the bed and stared down at a very fine silver watch. His jaw twitched as he pulled his gaze away. Clearly the gentry had gotten to Mr. Smallwood and asked him to lie. He was no longer a credible witness, and therefore a waste of his time. "It has naught to do with it, Mr. Smallwood." Thomas reached down and lifted the watch, examining it carefully. He only held it a few moments before it was snatched from his hand. "Tis a very fine watch, Mr. Smallwood. Where did you acquire it?"

His lip was curled in a snarl as he tucked the watch into his pocket. "Twas a gift from a friend."

Thomas nodded slowly. A friend indeed. Mr. Garrett must have been in such a great hurry he had not noticed there was a small note that hugged the bottom of the watch. He now had proof Mr. Garrett had paid Mr. Smallwood handsomely. Now if only someone else could place Mr. Garrett at the scene, or give him a reason why he would have murdered Mr. Purcell, he could approach the judge on Mrs. Purcell's behalf. "Thank you for your time. I will come pay you another visit if there is anything else I require."

Betty walked up the steps of the Murray household. Where Francis's home had been wide and plain, Thomas's house was small but grand. The wooden trim adorning the windows and every plane were extravagant and utterly beautiful. She did not feel quite as nervous approaching this house, and she was not sure why.

After a knock and few beats, a servant answered the door. She was well dressed, her apron white and crisp and tidy. "Good day," she said.

"Good day," Betty replied. "I was hoping Madam Murray was available. I have come to discuss some business."

The servant opened the door and stepped aside, allowing Betty in. The wooden floors beneath her feet were very much unlike those at her own home, however these floors looked clean and smelled of lavender. She was shown to the waiting room, which was decorated in a very lively shade of pink. The dark furniture popped against the cream trim that adorned the edges of the room, and there were windows on both the front wall and the right wall.

She stood beside one window and looked out onto the bustling street. She could imagine the English streets would be much busier. She'd read their population was quite a deal greater than that of the colonies.

Betty glanced around and wondered what it would be like to be the lady of such a grand house. She wondered how many servants Madam Murray had, and if she ever cooked a meal herself. She wondered how often they entertained guests. Though they most likely never entertained guests of her station.

The door creaked softly open and Betty spun to face Madam Murray. Her breath caught in her throat when she saw Thomas standing there instead. He did not fit into this room at all. He should have been surrounded by blues and browns, though the pink background did give him somewhat of a fantastical appearance. He was a fantasy. He would never belong to her in any way other than friendship. And even that would be cut short too soon when she left for England.

"Good day, Betty. I spotted you walking up the steps. You've come to discuss things with my mother?"

Betty nodded and clasped her hands in front of her. She was nervous he had second thoughts. Did he wish her to leave? Was he merely being kind, and the suggestion had been one she should not have entertained? Her stomach began to flutter. "That is what you told me to do, is it not?"

"Tis. However..." He pulled at his cravat as if it were choking him, his eyes leaving her for a moment before coming back. "I'm afraid I may have misjudged the severity of the sewing."

A pain crushed Betty's chest. Was this going to be a repeat of Mrs. Garrett and her harsh words? She wasn't sure she could stay to find out. "I see," she said, and could not hide the disappointment in her voice. "I should take leave then."

He caught her arm before she could move past him, every nerve on her skin sung at his touch. She gasped and looked up at him. He was looking down at her as if he were a man pained, his breath coming hard. Her eyes widened in surprise as his lips slowly dropped towards hers. He stopped himself, his honey-colored eyes frantically searching hers. Searching for what, she was unclear. She could only guess it was for approval.

She inched her lips forward and closed her eyes. They were but a breath's width apart when the door opened once more. Thomas set her from him so quickly she tipped the tea tray over. Her cheeks flushed, heated from the near kiss and the embarrassment of his actions.

“Thomas? What are you doing in here? Did Joan misunderstand our visitor’s demands?”

Thomas shoved a hand through his hair before shaking his head. “No, Mother. This is Betty Paca.” He stepped aside so that she would be revealed.

“Betty Paca. And what has she done for you to thrust her across the room? Has she tried to press her lips to yours again?”

Thomas mumbled something to himself before answering. “No, Mother. She was attempting to leave without speaking with you.”

His mother stepped aside and regarded her. “What business did you have with me this day, Miss Paca?”

Betty curtsied and then spoke. “I purchased a dress without permission from my father and I wish to earn the coin to replace what he had to spend on it. I have been cutting leathers for the shoe maker but I lost some.”

“Are you scatterbrained?”

“No, madam.”

“Mother.” Thomas warned and Betty felt her cheeks flush deeper. Thomas’s protection of her sent warmth to her belly.

His mother shrugged a shoulder and went to sit on the settee. She nodded to a seat across the room, and Betty sat. "I was just inquiring. Leathers would seem to be a hard thing to lose."

"I was running," Betty said.

"Running? Why ever for? Was an animal chasing you?"

Betty paused as she considered the answer to the question. "I suppose you could say it was an animal chasing me, yes."

"Does this have to do with the gossip I heard about mud upon Madam Garrett's face and carriage?"

Betty dropped her eyes guiltily, which caused Mrs. Murray to laugh.

"Whatever it was said between you, I have no doubt she deserved far worse than some dirt upon her face. I finished up the sewing last evening and I have a large number of servants to help with daily tasks." Her eyes moved over Betty, causing her grave concern the longer it went on. "Leave us, Thomas."

When he did not move, his mother turned her eyes to him. He grumbled but showed himself out the door, leaving them alone.

"Do you have designs on my son, Miss Paca?"

She was shocked at the question. Shocked she was even having to debate what the proper answer would be. "Your son is most kind and generous, Madam."

"Yes, he is. And I fear he may be too kind to some."

"Me, you mean."

"Miss Paca I've heard of your father's current status. I know he has procured travel across the sea back to England. I do not want my son to be hurt when he finds himself on the dock, staring at the ship that has you on board."

Betty was stunned at this as well. Why would Thomas be hurt if she left? He had all but told her he had no desire to kiss her. He had shown no interest in anything aside from friendship save for a moment ago, when he was most likely confused or not quite as awake as he normally was when they called upon each other.

"Madam, I mean no disrespect, but I feel safe to say I could not hurt Thomas even if I desired to do so."

"While I do believe that is your honest feeling, Miss Paca, I do not believe you know the power you yield over him. I will give you work, Miss Paca, an opportunity to give your father back what you spent, but you must promise to stay away from my son."

Her lips pressed together in worry. "Madam, I assure you I do not seek him out. I have no designs to marry your son."

"Excellent," Mrs. Murray said, clapping her hands in front of her chest tightly. "Then you will not mind what I am to ask you."

Betty waited patiently, her mind searching for what it could possibly be.

"Miss Paca, my son is of the age where he needs a wife. His father wishes to see him married to a good woman before he passes away and it won't be long now before he leaves this Earth. I will pay you a very decent sum of coin if you can find him a gentry woman, I know you are close to the bunch of them, and persuade him to propose to one of them. If you can manage to pull this off before you leave, I will pay you handsomely. And if you cannot... then you will have to find another way to pay your father back for your indiscretions."

"Why do you have need of me?" she asked, confused. Surely it would not be difficult for Thomas to find himself a wife.

"Because he speaks fondly of you, Miss Paca, and I believe your opinion means a great deal to him. Much more than my own."

Betty stared down at her hands as she considered the offer. She could try to convince one of her friends to marry Thomas, but she wasn't sure which one would suit him best. Sally was too flighty, she would drive Thomas to drink. Anne was still not over the loss of her beau to her sister. That left Lydia, Charlotte, and Elizabeth. She cleared her throat softly before responding. "I need some time to consider the proposition, Madam Murray."

Mrs. Murray nodded as she stood from her seat. "Of course. Send word to me should you choose to accept the offer and don't wait too long. I know the ships have been late to the harbor but they will come, and as you sail away so does your chance at a small dowry that you may offer to a suitor who fancies you."

Betty stood up and curtsied, before leaving the house. She was crossing the intersection when a warm hand on her elbow pulled her backwards. She tried to tug away, noticing the hand belonged to Francis. He sneered down at her.

"Where are you off to, Miss Paca? My mother's house is the other way."

"Release me at once!" Betty said, loudly, hoping to draw attention to them.

He flashed her a slimy smile. "I do not think so. Not until you have apologized to my mother for your behavior the other day." He pulled her roughly to his chest. "Or would you prefer a different kind of punishment?"

The way his eyes darkened brought a flash of fear into her chest. She had no idea what was playing on in his head, but she wasn't sure she wanted to find out. "Release me," she said again, keeping her chin high. It was broad daylight and she was well liked in the town. He would not be able to do whatever he pleased with her.

"Going to play difficult, are you?" he asked as his fingertips clasped one of her loose strands and traced it from her scalp to the tip. "I like my women feisty." His gaze roamed over her chest and made her feel unclean. She tried to tug away, but he held her tightly. "Tell me, Betty, how many men have—"

He did not finish his sentence before he was pulled away, and his nose met with a fist.

Once Betty was released, she started running. She did not wish to see who had come to save her until she was a safe distance away. The commotion on the street was greater now two men of the gentry were coming to fists. From the back, Francis's coal-dark hair was wild. And Thomas, a dash of red blood aside his lips, gripped the edge of his coat and pulled it taut. His eyes lifted to hers and color bloomed on her cheeks. She would have to find a way to thank him for saving her. And she needed to be more diligent about not going around town alone. She was not sure when or if Francis would strike again.

Chapter Thirteen

Thomas entered the shoemaker's shop and waited while he finished with his current customer. He glanced around at the piles of shoes hanging from the ceiling. He doubted he would find what he was looking for up there, actually hoping he did not, otherwise his hunch would be much harder to prove.

None of the shoes had anything engraved into the soles. He had been to three different shoemakers' this morning. This was the last in town, and therefore his last hope of chasing down this lead.

When they were alone, Thomas smiled and approached. "Good day. I am inquiring about a set of footprints I have seen in the streets. I was hoping to have my own pair commissioned, and I was wondering if it were you who crafted the pair that I saw."

"Tis possible."

"It was the most unusual thing that I have ever laid eyes upon," he said. "There were markings on the heels."

"Ah, yes. I have commissioned shoes like those before. I have one customer who only wishes to have carved soles exclusively."

"You do?"

"Yes, Mr. Garrett and his wife have been ordering special shoes for at least two years past."

He nodded, hiding the churning in his gut well. Mr. Garrett had not been on the top of his list, his son had been. If Mr. Garrett and his wife were responsible then...

"Did you wish to place an order, sir?"

"I am still considering. Did Mr. Garrett ever purchase these for his son, sir?"

The shop owner considered for a moment before nodding his head. "I do believe so. His son was rather unhappy and had them returned." The shop keeper walked around his crowded workspace, picking up scraps of leather, half constructed shoes, and papers, until he pulled out a pair of boots, muddied and well worn.

"Might I see them?" Thomas inquired. When the shoemaker handed them over, Thomas inspected them carefully, his eyes taking in the symbol on the bottom of the shoe first. He nodded as he set them down on the counter. It was a match. Francis has been at the Purcell's house. "When did he return them? They seem very well worn."

The shoemaker grumbled something before scratching the back of his head. "The days run together, sir. I am not sure. Recently."

Thomas nodded. "Would you be willing to testify to this information in the courts?"

The shoemaker's brows furrowed. "Sir, I cannot afford to stop production to spend a day in the courts."

"You will be compensated, sir, I personally will see to it."

The shoemaker took the boots back and gave him a nod. "I suppose I could come tell them what I know."

"That would be very helpful. Thank you. I will expect to see you in court in a few days for Mrs. Purcell's hearing."

The shoemaker absorbed the implication, and gave a nod. "Yes. Sir. Good day."

Thomas pulled coin from his coat pocket and set it onto the well-worn wooden counter. "On second thought, I would like to purchase the pair of boots." The shoemaker's eyes assessed the coin but made no move to hand over the shoes. Thomas tripled the coin and nodded at it. "Worn boots will not fetch a finer coin than this, sir." Thomas did not offer him much time to consider his offer. He lifted his hand and reached for the coin, but it swiftly disappeared, and a pair of used boots landed on the counter beside Thomas's hand. With a nod of his head and a self-serving smile, he retrieved them and made haste to his office.

The judge refused to meet with Thomas and prompted him to write down his grievances and leave it with his secretary, Mr. Wythe. Upon receipt, Mr. Wythe glanced at the lengthy handwritten note and set it aside. There was no telling if or when the judge might receive the note. Thomas had been hoping to avoid Mrs. Purcell going to court at all as she was only accused by circumstances. He had failed Mrs. Purcell. With a heavy heart, Thomas walked down the streets until he was standing in front of the Raleigh Tavern. He had not eaten all day, and his spirits could not be much lower. He stepped inside, intent on having a full belly of food and ale when he stepped out again.

Betty was standing in front of her window with Mr. Blue Bell in her arms. She had made a decision about Thomas. She would speak with him, and if he would care for a wife then she would do what she could to find him one before she left. Not only for the money, but also to thank him for what he'd done for her.

She hadn't spoken to her father about the incident. She was sure he would only tell Betty she'd surely deserved it for being so disrespectful to Mrs. Garrett. He was still not speaking with her, still giving her the silent treatment for trying to ignite sparks between himself and Madam McDowell. It suited Betty just fine, however, because if he ignored her, she couldn't feel badly for not telling him what had been going on in her life. She had never before been so involved in so many different circles.

The kitten glanced outside and mewed loudly a few times, signaling all too well what its intensions were. She moved with Mr. Blue Bell to the front door and let him out into the street. She watched for a moment before a male voice spoke from the darkness. "I had hoped you would come out some time."

She let out a scream of surprise, but it was muffled before she could finish. She thrashed against the arms that held her until she realized it was Thomas.

"Shh," he said, his breath tainted with drink.

She turned around and slapped him across his cheek. She was shocked at the sting in her hand—she'd never before slapped a man. Even though it was dark, the moonlight illuminated his cheek well enough that she saw the pink impression of her palm. She fought the urge to apologize. He deserved it for sneaking up on her in the darkness and scaring her half to death.

"I take it I thoroughly surprised you," he said as he rubbed his face.

"What are you doing here at this time of night, Thomas?" She glanced around to see if anyone else was around, they were not.

"I just happened to be passing by."

"Coming from a tavern if the smell of you is any judge."

"Do I smell that badly?" He lifted his coat and sniffed it.

She gently pulled his coat down. "Yes. Stop that. If someone were to see you..."

"Then what? Betty." He slurred his words slightly as he closed the distance between them. She backed up until she was flush against the side of her house. His nearness made her glad for the sturdy support it offered.

"Thank you," she said quickly, her eyes wide as she stared up at him.

His eyes wandered over her features, now that he was closer she could see the swollen corner of his lip and the purple bruise aside his cheek. "I am not sure I deserve your thanks."

"For handling Mr. Garrett," she said.

"Ah. Yes, well, it was what any gentleman would have done. It deserves no special consideration."

"Thomas... are you ready for a wife? Would a wife make you happy?"

"A wife? I suppose a certain kind of wife could make me happy."

"What kind of wife?"

His eyes searched hers for a moment before his face scrunched up in confusion. "Wh-How am I to answer that, Betty?"

She pressed her fingers against the house, they were itching to reach up and touch him. But she held them down. She needed the money to pay off her debts, she reminded herself. And falling in love with Thomas, kissing Thomas was not going to solve her problems. With her focus now firmly back in place she asked, "What would your wife look like? What kind of woman are you attracted to?"

His words were slow and drawn out. "Dark hair, lips plump like pillows."

She made a mental note of his response and then, "And her qualities?"

"Kind. Bold. Someone to make me stop and appreciate little things."

"Little things?" she asked, perplexed at this statement. Did he have someone in mind? Someone she and his mother knew nothing of?

He nodded and his body drew closer to hers. She saw where his lips were headed and she ducked under his arm and put distance between them again. She would not allow Thomas Murray to kiss her while under the influence of alcohol, despite how desperately she might feel like she might want to kiss him. He was not in his right mind.

"You should be heading home, Mr. Murray, while you still can."

He rested his head against the side of her home and let out a deep sigh. "Yes. I suppose you are correct in your assessment. You would make a good wife, Betty."

A laugh bubbled from her chest. "You know that would not be the case, Mr. Murray. I spend my father's money without asking, I am reckless with my emotions and actions as a result."

"You have spirit. Your husband would never tire from boredom."

"Your wife would be lucky to share your last name, your wealth, your power, and position."

He pushed off the house and stuffed his hand into his pockets. "Is that what interests you, Betty? Wealth? Power? Position?" His eyes darkened and she took in a sharp breath, "If that is so, you should have allowed Francis Garret to fondle you in the street for everyone to see. Your father could force him to take your hand if you were with child. Then your prayers would be answered and you could stay in Williamsburg until your death."

She said nothing, she did not wish to anger him further, nor did she wish to refute his feelings. It was clear he would not remember much of what came from his lips this evening. And with the realization was another; she would have to speak her apology to him again in the light of day.

"Good evening, Betty."

She watched him stagger down the road until he was but a small dot on the horizon. Mr. Blue Bell's rub against her skirts and loud purr pulled her attention away. She scooped him up and headed back into the house for the evening.

Chapter Fourteen

There was a knock on his door and Thomas sighed as he set his quill into the pot.

"Yes? Come in."

The last person he'd expected to see came in through his office door. He stood as she entered and looked her over, then behind her. He did not see another escort and cursed her under his breath. She either had the shortest memory known to humankind or she felt like she was invincible. Thomas knew Francis Garrett and what he was capable of. And he knew now that Betty had rejected his advances she would be at the top of his list of acquisitions.

The previous evening played back in his mind and he batted away his feelings and concern for her.

"Good day, Mr. Murray." She offered him a curtsy

and came to his desk, a basket hanging from her arm. "I wanted to formally thank you for stepping in with Mr. Garrett yesterday." She set the basket on his desk and lifted the corner. A display of tartlets winked at him before she drew the cloth back across it.

His jaw clenched. He wished desperately he could accept them, offer her a smile, but if he gave her the wrong impression it would be his heart that would be crushed.

"If you really did care to thank me, Miss Paca, you would have brought along an escort. For my effort yesterday would have been wasted if he were to attack you again. Or perhaps that was your intent?"

The hurt evident in her gaze did give him a slight bit of satisfaction. She seemed disagreeable to the idea of Francis touching her. Almost as disagreeable as he felt about it.

He came around his desk and took her by the elbow, perhaps more roughly than he had anticipated. "Come, was this your only errand?"

"No, I was going to pay a visit to my friend Charlotte Greene."

"Is she expecting you?"

"No."

As much as he wanted to send her in his carriage, he was afraid she would leave Charlotte's house unaccompanied as well.

"Come, we will take my carriage."

"We?" she asked, pulling back as he tugged her towards the door.

"Yes."

"I did not wish to pull you from your work, Thomas. I am capable of walking to Charlotte's house on my own."

"Capable, yes. And also the target of a certain gentleman who has very savage designs on you. Until he finds another woman to prey upon, you need to walk with an escort. If I discover you continuing to go out alone, I will have to speak with your father, Betty." He stopped and turned her so she was facing him, his hands on her arms, holding her firmly so she would look at him. "This is serious, Betty."

"He is Francis Garrett, Mr. Murray. He is not some monster in a child's fairy tale."

He clenched his jaw tightly and resisted the urge to shake the nonsense from her. She did not know, no one did. And Thomas could tell no one, for who would believe Mr. Garrett's son capable of such things? "He is every bit a monster from a child's fairy tale. I can see your defiance will be a hindrance to you. You leave me no choice but to discuss this with your father."

"No," she pleaded, her hands going to his arms, gripping them tight. The shocks that went through his body at her touch startled him. He swallowed hard against it.

Don't be stupid, Thomas.

"I swear I will not go out again without an escort."

He studied her eyes and when he was convinced she was speaking the truth, he nodded and released her. "I will take you to Charlotte's residence. And I will leave if you promise to have her escort you home."

She nodded. "Yes, Thomas, I promise."

He leaned down and pressed a kiss to her forehead. His lips rested there for a moment too long. When he pulled away, she was staring up at him expectantly. He'd let his guard down again and done something foolish. He turned and left her standing in the middle of the entryway. No matter how far Betty Paca got into his heart, he would resist her. His mother would never approve, and he did not wish her to be hurt that way. She did not deserve it.

Chapter Fifteen

Thomas followed her out of the carriage and to the front door.

"You do not need to stay beside me, Thomas."

"I need to be sure she is home to receive your call, Miss Paca."

Betty sighed and turned back to the door. They stood side by side and said nothing. It was as quiet as the carriage ride had been. She hadn't wanted Thomas to speak with her father and she was furious he'd trapped her into the ridiculous agreement. She was not a child, she did not need an escort.

She wanted to inquire about Francis and why Thomas thought so ill of him, but she didn't want to open that wound either, and she was almost certain Thomas would say nothing about why he felt that way. Perhaps he was envious of Francis's newly appointed station to the House of Burgesses.

The door swung open and a servant greeted them.

"What business do you have this day?" the servant asked, looking between Betty and Thomas expectantly.

Betty turned to Thomas and curtsied. "Good day, Mr. Murray."

"Is Charlotte home and able to receive callers?" Thomas asked, ignoring Betty's curtsy.

"Yes, sir."

Thomas looked at Betty and bowed. "Good day, then, Miss Paca. Perhaps I shall see you this evening at the ball."

When he was out of earshot, she revealed her reason for calling. "I wish to call upon Charlotte Greene to discuss a possible suitor," Betty said. The servant ushered her into the waiting room. It was a few minutes before Charlotte swept into the room.

"Betty!" They hugged and sat down opposite each other. "Would you care for tea?"

"Yes, thank you."

After the tea was served and they had gotten past the small talk, Betty set down her cup and saucer. "Do you have your sights sets on a suitor?"

"I had not really considered it, I suppose," she

said with a shrug of her slender shoulders. "And you? Is there someone who has caught your fancy, Betty?"

"No," she said, shaking her head. "Do you remember the man I danced with?"

"The one you kissed and scared from the ballroom?"

Betty blushed and nodded. "Yes. That one."

"Yes, Thomas Murray. His father owns a large tobacco plantation and several buildings in town. The rumor has it his father has invested well despite his being bed-ridden. And once he passes, Thomas will be extremely well off and very well to do."

Betty nodded. "Yes, his father has done quite well with his investments. And..." She leaned forward and lowered her voice. "Madam Murray has told me in confidence her husband is not doing well and wishes to see Thomas married before he passes."

Charlotte set her cup down slowly. "Are you saying that you think Thomas and I would make a good match?"

Betty nodded after a bit of hesitation. "Why would you not? He has told me in confidence that he desires a wife with dark hair, supple lips, a kind and bold heart. And I swear that describes you perfectly. I think he is not as comfortable with courting as other gentlemen are."

"Betty, I admit it does sound a bit like me. But he could equally have been describing you."

Betty's heart pounded in her ears and her palms were suddenly damp. The thought of Thomas describing herself as his perfect woman was one she enjoyed too much. She shook her head emphatically as she pressed a hand to her chest. "No. He has expressed no interest in me, Charlotte. I was hoping you would dance with him at the upcoming ball and see if there is a love interest between you."

Charlotte tilted her head as she considered it. "I suppose it would not hurt to have a dance or two with Mr. Murray. Are you certain he fancies me?"

"I know no other women dark of hair with supple lips, my dear friend."

Charlotte's lips broke into a wide grin. "Oh, but my dreams will be pleasantly filled until the ball."

Betty smiled in return but deep in her heart something was not right. Was she jealous of her friend? It was a ridiculous notion. "I am so glad I could bring you such sweet dreams. I must go, I have someone else I need to call upon today. Will I see you this evening at the ball?"

Charlotte nodded as she stood. As they parted ways, Betty could hear the echo of Thomas's warning.

He is the monster of child's fairy tales, Betty.

She shook her head as she left Charlotte's town

home and walked down the dusty streets towards Mrs. Murray's home. She would tell her at once she would accept the proposition. And then she would go to Francis's home and apologize to his mother. Perhaps then Thomas would stop following her like a sheep dog herding a sheep.

There was a tray set up nearby for two. Betty had been sitting in the sitting room for what would be considered a very indecent amount of time. If Mrs. Garrett did not come through the door soon, Betty would have to leave and come back another day. The afternoon sun was slowly on its way towards the ground and she had one more call to make and a ball to prepare for.

A part of her wished that Mrs. Garrett would not appear. If she did not appear then Betty could leave and in her defense could say she attempted to sit with her and it had not come to pass. She was staring at the door and counting to twenty. At fifteen the door swung open and Mrs. Garrett appeared. She stopped short just inside the door and stared at Betty.

"Open your hands," she said, staring down at Betty's closed fists.

Betty glanced down and watched as she forced her hands to relax and open.

Mrs. Garrett sniffed and stuck her nose into the air. "No mud, I see."

Betty dipped her eyes. "That is why I have come to visit, Mrs. Garrett. I am so sincerely sorry for my behavior the other day. I do not know what came over me. My father says a spirit has come over me since... well, there are going to be changes in my life soon, Mrs. Garrett."

"Get stuck with a child, have you? And who is the father? That Mr. Murray?"

Betty's eyes shot to Mrs. Garrett's and she quickly shook her head. She did not need Mr. Murray caught up in gossip that surrounded her. She was trying to find him a good wife, not a forced wedding in her kitchen. "No, Mrs. Garrett. I assure you save for immaculate conception there would be no babe in my belly."

Mrs. Garrett sniffed again, something about her looked somewhat disappointed at the news. "Hm. Is that all you've come to say? I have errands I need to run in town. Can I be assured there will be no assault today?"

"Not from me, Madam."

"It most likely took a great deal of courage for you to come here and apologize. I appreciate your gesture, but please do not mistake my kindness for an invitation to acknowledge our very distant acquaintance."

Betty nodded. "Yes, madam." She had not foreseen herself ever wanting to stop on the street and have a chat with Mrs. Garrett, but if that idea had ever come to pass she now knew she should dismiss it in kind.

"Very well. The maid will see you out. Good day." With a nod of her chin, she swept herself from the room once again. It was as if she had never been there at all.

Betty stood and before she could make it to the door the maid entered and approached. Betty paused when the maid did not veer, and when the maid's hands went to her clothes Betty quickly stepped away.

"I beg your pardon."

"Sorry, miss. Mrs. Garrett wishes me to search you for stolen goods."

"Whatever would I have stolen?"

The maid looked at Betty, pity in her expression. "I do not know, miss, perhaps some cutlery or a precious family heirloom. Please raise your arms so I may feel for foreign objects."

Betty was humiliated as the maid ran her hands along the length of her body. Mrs. Garrett was standing in the doorway observing, a grin on her lips. When she was finished the maid stepped aside and Betty kept her eyes to the ground as she left the house. She would never understand people like Mrs. Garrett who abused their power and money just because they were able.

"Good day," Mrs. Garrett called with a grin in her voice.

Once she'd returned home, Betty went up to her room and cried on her bed. She would have preferred a face full of mud to a stranger touching her body. She beat herself up thinking she wanted to be married to that woman's son. She had seen nothing but Francis's looks, and his wealth, and his power. Betty felt she deserved the humiliation she'd received for being so blind to who Francis really was.

The ball was going to start when the sun lowered and she needed to put herself right.

"Do not continue to pity yourself, Betty," she said aloud. "You will not make the mistake again. You will go with your father to England and you will marry for love, true love, not because of a handsome, charming smile."

Her mind went to Thomas. He was probably just the same as Francis. Their mothers were similar. While Francis's mother was more vindictive and perhaps had a less pure heart, Thomas's mother was still very concerned with station and wealth. Betty doubted she would ever be good enough in Mrs. Murray's mind. Not that Betty was even thinking of marrying Thomas. It was just that Thomas needed to marry, so it was on her mind. She pushed all thoughts of that away for the time being and concentrated on dressing for the ball.

Just as she was about to leave, her father came in through the front door. "Betty." He sounded as surprised as he looked to see her. His eyes took in the red silk dress and she couldn't help but sense the sadness in his eyes. For both of them, this dress was the reason her mother's last possessions had been sold away.

"Father. I will return before morning."

He looked as if he might have something else to say but decided against it.

Chapter Sixteen

When Betty entered the ballroom she instantly searched the familiar faces around her. There were a few gentlemen she didn't know, probably visitors from the Northern Colonies, but most of those gathered were familiar.

She walked the perimeter of the room until she was standing amongst her friends who were discussing the latest in Paris fashions. When Betty met Charlotte's eye, she nodded outside their circle, letting her know she wished to speak with her privately. Charlotte gracefully moved away from her friends and took Betty by the arm.

"One dance with your Thomas?" she asked, her eyes bouncing around the room as they conspired.

"He is not *my* Thomas," Betty insisted.

Charlotte chuckled softly, her eyes still searching for him. "Neither is he mine."

"He could very well be. Dance with him as much as you wish."

Charlotte studied Betty's solemn face and nodded. "Very well. Have you seen him?"

They cast their eyes to the crowd, sizing up each of the men that their gazes fell upon.

"Oh, there he is," Charlotte said, nodding in the direction of the ballroom entrance.

Betty's breath stuttered in her throat as she took in the sight of him. His dark coat accentuated his broad shoulders very well. It was all she could do not to stare at him and take in the rest of his appearance. Her knees shook, thinking of what she must do. She reminded herself once more of the money and the plan. She was doing this for Madam Murray.

"Come on," Betty said, pushing her feelings away, she took hold of Charlotte's hand and tugged until they were standing before Thomas.

Thomas smiled at Betty, his eyes taking in her red dress, as if he had not seen it less than a fortnight prior. He bowed. "Miss Paca. Good evening."

Betty curtsied, it was the polite thing to do. She tried to ignore the way his roaming eyes made her heart flutter. "Mr. Murray. I wish to introduce Miss Charlotte Greene to you."

Charlotte curtsied low and Betty couldn't help but notice her friend's plunging neckline. Betty wondered how her bosom stayed in place. But when she snuck a peak at Thomas, his eyes were firmly on Betty's. She felt herself blush. Why was he staring at her and not at the lovely bosom at her side?

Thomas, looking satisfied for a reason unknown to Betty, took ahold of Charlotte's hand and pressed a soft kiss to the back of her glove. "A pleasure, Miss Greene. We have met before, but perhaps not had such a proper introduction."

"Charlotte was hoping to dance with you, Mr. Murray," Betty said. Her brain had been too slow to jump in any earlier. It was stuttering at the sight of Thomas kissing another woman. Even if it were just Charlotte's glove, she wished it had been her own.

His eyes went from Charlotte to Betty, steely determination twinkling in them. "Is she? Does she not know that I do not dance?"

"She saw you dancing at the ball prior and was hoping, since I advised her of your superior skills, that you would indulge her as well."

He looked at Charlotte and winked. "So long as you do not kiss me as your friend did, then I would be honored to share a dance with you," Thomas said, holding out his arm.

Charlotte let out a little giggle, grabbed onto his

arm, and was escorted onto the dance floor. Betty watched them as they moved together and she wondered if she had looked as right in his arms as her friend did. She forced her gaze away just as Mrs. Murray came to stand next to her.

"This is a good match, Miss Paca. Are they well suited?"

"My friend is of good station, Mrs. Murray, if that is what you mean."

"Indeed that is part of it." She watched in silence for a moment. "He does seem to be enjoying himself, does he not?"

Thomas was smiling and whispering things in Charlotte's ear that made her laugh. His hands rested comfortably upon her lower back and clutched her hand with familiarity. Their bodies were pressed as tightly together as the movement of the waltz would allow. Betty swallowed the lump in her throat as she nodded, and pasted on a faux smile.

"Yes, Madam, he does. You must be very pleased."

She nodded. "Yes, if he speaks of her as much as he speaks of you, then I shall be very pleased indeed."

Her heart picked up speed once more, and she wished it would just choose a pace and stay there. She was afraid she would have to call for the doctor if it continued to be so erratic. "You are too kind, Madam."

"I only wish that I were, Miss Paca." Mrs. Murray's smile grew larger as her son approached the both of them, Charlotte still on his arm. "Hello, darling. I'm so glad you were able to pull yourself away from work long enough to make it."

Thomas looked to Charlotte with a smile. "As am I, Mother."

Charlotte's cheeks flushed, and a sharp stab of sickness hit Betty's gut.

"Wonderful. And who is this beautiful woman on your arm?"

Thomas made the introductions and Betty searched for a reason to sneak away from the party. She refused to stand idly by and listen to them gush about how wonderful Charlotte was. She *was* wonderful, but that was not the point of it. Betty desired for Thomas to speak that way of her. She wished he would compliment her impeccable dance form and gush to his mother about how graceful she was.

"Pardon me," Betty said finally, cutting Thomas off mid-sentence. "I must go find my own dance partner." She curtsied quickly and dashed away, refusing to look back as she headed for her circle of friends.

Anne was standing with her back to the wall, a cup of tea in her hands. "You look practically miserable, Betty Paca."

"I am feeling fine, Anne."

"Did Charlotte steal your beau?"

"No, she did not steal him. He twas not mine to start."

"Tis a shame," Anne continued. "I hear his father is on his death bed and Thomas will be inheriting a pretty penny rather soon."

"I gather that is why Charlotte is showing such interest in Thomas Murray. She once said she would not marry him, even if he were the last man in the colonies," Lydia said.

"Why would she say such a thing?" Betty inquired.

"She thinks him too plain," Lydia said with a shrug.

"Too plain?" Betty asked, turning her eyes to Thomas. She would argue he was anything but plain. He was intelligent, and thoughtful, and kind. His eyes were deep and harbored more emotions than she'd ever known a man could possess. And his lips, while they appeared to be hard as steel at times, were soft and inviting. Her improper thoughts flushed the surface of her cheeks.

"Yes, too plain. Charlotte wants to marry a dark haired man with blue eyes. She said she saw him in her dreams many times and that he is her destiny. But perhaps she's let go of those dreams and embraced new ones."

"Perhaps her mother has forced her to."

"Is she in need of a husband?" Betty asked.

"Oh, yes. Her father is nearly ruined. She needs a practical marriage. And soon."

This put a damper on the whole match Betty had set up. And if Charlotte only wanted to marry Thomas for his money and power, she could not allow that to happen. Unless he was prepared to love Charlotte, Betty could not let Thomas be tricked into marriage.

"Excuse me," Betty said. She grabbed up her red skirts and made a bee-line for Thomas and Charlotte. She paused a few feet away as she stared at the two of them. Serious Thomas was laughing and smiling, the lean of his body into Charlotte's space proving he was interested. He was happy, and who was she to take it away from him? Betty could not let her feelings of jealousy stand in the way of his happiness.

"They look happy, do they not?" Madam Murray asked. "You have done a fine job, indeed, Betty, of quickly finding a suitable match for Thomas. I will let my friends know you have a penchant for match-making and perhaps you may grow your wealth here in the colonies. For while we do not have all the free-doms men have, we women can still afford our own living."

Betty smiled softly, though her heart was aching

at the thought of staying in Williamsburg without a friendship with Thomas. "I do think that would be too kind. Your friends would likely be disappointed. Thomas spoke with me privately about his desires in a wife, and I merely listened. I do not think the process could be repeated."

"I do think perhaps you are too hard on yourself, Miss Paca."

Betty politely bowed her head and gave a small curtsy. "You must be right, Mrs. Murray. I do hope you will excuse me, I am feeling quite tired."

Mrs. Murray's brows furrowed. "Surely you would like to dance a bit. There are many eligible men here."

Betty smiled as she picked up her skirts. "I am afraid they will have to wait for another time." Or never, Betty thought gravely. She would never attend another ball in Williamsburg. In two days' time, she would sail across the ocean to England.

"I do hope you will come by tomorrow to collect your payment for your services."

The money. Betty swallowed hard, a large lump she was sure was guilt refused to move. "I apologize, Mrs. Murray, but you should not expect for me to collect payment. Thomas has not yet asked for Charlotte's hand in marriage, and I do not think I will remain in Williamsburg when that times arrives.

Most likely he will wait until the end of the season, as is expected. For Thomas is nothing if not proper."

Mrs. Murray considered Betty for a long moment, her eyes every bit as blue as her son's. She nodded tightly. "I admire your integrity, Miss Paca. Forget we even discussed a payment for arranging a marriage for Thomas."

"Thank you." She was about to ask if Mrs. Murray would be so kind as to keep her abreast on Thomas's status, but quickly closed her mouth, nodding instead to take her leave. She could keep in touch with Charlotte just as easily. Or Sally. As Betty moved towards the exit, she urgently fought the need to look back. She closed her eyes as she waited for the guests ahead of her to finish their goodbyes to the hosts of the ball.

She could still see Thomas, happy and smiling down at her friend. Charlotte would take care of him. She could make him very happy. She would be a good wife. As much as Betty didn't want to, she could leave Williamsburg at least knowing that Thomas's happiness had been secured.

Chapter Seventeen

Thomas turned down the lamplight until darkness was cloaked over his office. He had not intended to stay so late, but after his argument with his mother about what he'd overheard her saying to Betty, he could not return home. It was just as well, he had a case to present in the morning.

He covered his yawn with his fist and gathered his things. He'd sent his driver away long ago so he had a walk ahead of him.

He fast approached the Raleigh Tavern and the loud voices drew his attention. He paused, wondering if a tankard of ale would satisfy the empty feeling inside of him. Charlotte was a lovely woman, and very talented in the art of flirtation, but he had no desire to court her. The woman he thought he'd wished to court was scheming with his own mother. His work had done a decent enough job of distracting him, but the conversation he'd heard between them had frequently come bounding into his mind.

A few things had surprised him. Firstly, that Betty had turned down his mother's offer of payment. It had been his idea that she seek out work from his own mother, for he knew how badly she'd needed the funds. Secondly, she had not stayed after declining the payment. Without the sum to buy her more time, he would have expected her to go flitting into the arms of Francis Garrett, or one of his friends, to try and desperately find a way to marry one of them, as is what she truly wanted.

And the largest question of all: why had she not put herself into his path? Why had she chosen Charlotte? He could have sworn he'd seen the light of jealousy in her eyes as he'd held onto her friend. It was the only reason he'd kept on with the ruse, he was sad to admit it. Perhaps she truly had no desire to marry him.

He thought of the last time he'd partaken in the tavern, his drunken near-kiss with Betty. He shook his head and decided against entering, he did not wish to repeat his offense to Betty. He needed his wits about him tomorrow in court and if he spent the good part of the evening drinking, he would have to fight against a cloud in the morning.

The hair rose on the back of his neck as a group of men seemed to come from the shadows and surrounded him.

"Mr. Murray. What a pleasant surprise."

Thomas slowed his steps, and finally stopped. His jaw clenched tightly. Francis stood behind the men in the shadows, a leery smile on his lips.

"Mr. Garrett. The surprise is not as strong for me. I knew it would not be long before the snake appeared from the shadows."

Francis stayed at a distance as the men, no doubt hired, started to close in around Thomas. He closed his eyes tightly, knowing that fighting them off would be impossible and possibly fatal.

"A snake? Come, Thomas, snakes are primal, simple. I am methodical, purposeful. Much like the savages who used to surround our grandfather's in the woods. Unlike them, however, I will win."

Thomas shook his head, his fist tight on the leather satchel at his side that held the notice of Mrs. Purcell's release. Insufficient evidence against her. "I know it was you, Francis. I know you are the one who slaughtered Mr. Purcell. I am not the only one who knows it."

"You are the only one who will speak out against me, Thomas Murray. Or would have. Why do you think we are all here? You, my dear stupid neighbor, have to be taken care of."

"You will not get away with this."

"Only time shall tell. I do not think my peers would find me guilty of such a heinous crime."

"You have them fooled, for now."

"Hurry before someone comes by," Francis scolded.

The men closed in. A punch to his stomach left him unable to retort or yell as his breath left his lungs. A brute force on his spine dropped him to the muddied foul-smelling ground, where men had urinated, lost their stomachs, and worse.

While fists and feet pummeled him, his only thoughts were of Betty. He might never get to kiss her. He would not be able to protect her. He could never tell her how he truly felt. He must have spoken her name when it was all over, for Francis leaned down beside Thomas's ear and chuckled. "Fear not, Thomas. I will take care of Betty. Very good care of her."

He struggled against the pain, commanding his limbs to function and lift him from the ground, but they could not.

The visions of Thomas's subconscious tortured him with the thoughts of what Francis might do to Betty as the world around Thomas went black.

Betty woke to loud knocks on the front door and glanced out of her window. Darkness still cloaked Williamsburg. She heard her father get up and run below stairs. Her kitten was on guard as well, staring at the doorway.

"Mr. Paca, I am so sorry to bother you so late. Is your daughter Betty at home?"

Betty swung her legs out of bed at her name.

"Mrs. McDowell, it is very late. Come on, what are you doing here at this hour?"

Betty threw on her clothes and paused at the top of the stairs, listening intently. What could she possibly want with her?

Mrs. McDowell's voice was low and soft and rather shaken. Betty could see from her spot that Mrs. McDowell pulled her shawl tightly over her shoulders before she spoke. "Something has happened at Raleigh Tavern."

A rush of worry settled into the pit of her stomach. There was only one man she'd known who fancied the Raleigh Tavern. Betty came rushing down the last of the steps and stopped in front of the dressmaker. Betty face was pinched with worry and her heart thrumming loudly in her ears. "Who is it, Mrs. McDowell?"

"Tis Mr. Murray. I would have helped him if I could, but there was no one else about."

"Why did you not call the sheriff?" her father demanded, his voice gruffer than usual because of the hour.

Betty slipped her shoes and cape on quickly. "Because, Father, the men who did it most likely were dangerous, or perhaps she did not see them. It does not matter, does it? I must go help him."

Her father grabbed onto her arm as she attempted to leave the house. "Tis not safe for you to be out alone, nor Mrs. McDowell. Let me dress."

Betty nodded and hated there was a prickle of tears in her eyes. Thinking of Thomas, lying on the streets, possibly suffering and soon to die, did not sit well in her heart. "Hurry, Father, please."

Mrs. McDowell led them around the back of the tavern and there Thomas was, laying face up on the dirt, the tavern keeper standing over him. The tavern keeper stood and shook his head as they approached. "I did not get a good look at any of the hoodlums. I wasn't notified until after they were nearly finished with him. I've sent for the gaoler."

Her father took him aside and spoke with him, while Betty approached Thomas. His handsome face was so tattered it was hard to know it was him. Tears began to fall from her eyes. She could not help but feel responsible. There was only one person she knew who would be capable of such a thing, and who had reason to take his wrath out on Thomas. Thomas had stepped in for her with Francis, and was now suffering the consequences and taking the brunt of the punishment Francis had promised her.

Carefully she smoothed his hair back from his face. He groaned softly at the touch, but did not open his eyes. She was unsure if he even could, they were swollen to the size of apples.

"I am so sorry, Thomas," she whispered, her throat thick with the misery of it all.

Her father came up behind her and touched her shoulder. "The gaoler is on his way. I've sent Mrs. McDowell to fetch the physician. We should send for his family. Come. The tavern keeper will watch over him until we return."

"Can you not go without me?" she asked, not wanting to leave his side. What if the men returned? What if Francis's charming smile disarmed the tavern keeper, and Francis hurt Thomas further?

"I will not leave you here unattended. There is

obviously something sinister lurking in the shadows. Come."

With much hesitation, she stood up and followed her father. He wrapped an arm around her and pulled her to the Murray residence. The house was unlit and quiet. It took many knocks on the door before a servant answered, still dressed in his night-clothes.

"Yes? How can I help you?"

"Mr. Murray has been injured. A band of men pummeled him quite badly. Could you please inform his mother and father?"

"They are still at the ball but should be returning shortly. I will make sure Mr. Murray's bed is made up, and I will send for the town physician at once. Is Mr. Murray... is he able to walk?"

Her father shook his head. "No. Do you have a carriage? He will need a ride. I will assist with getting him in and out of it."

The servant shook his head. "Thank you for informing us, sir. We shall handle it from here."

"Father, please, let me stay with him."

Betty's father looked down at her and searched her face. "Tis not a good idea, Betty. Is he the man you have been courting? Is he the reason I have a wild animal indoors?"

She nodded slowly. "He did give me the kitten,

Father. But we are not courting. He does not feel as I do."

The servant was still standing in the doorway, listening.

Her father shook his head. "No, Betty, tis not decent. You can visit him during the day light hours like any other proper person. But you cannot stay with him overnight, unless you wish to be married when his lips are healed enough to agree to it."

The thought of marrying Thomas made her heart beat wildly in her chest. While she knew this would solve her dilemma about going overseas to England, she also knew Thomas was actively seeking a wife and she wanted nothing more than for him to be happy. While it hurt her deeply to think she may never see him again, that perhaps Madam Murray would not want her to be around her son, she nodded, agreeing with her father's demands. "I understand, Father."

With a heavy heart, Betty followed after her father as he insisted in keeping her at his side while he tended to getting Mr. Murray from the tavern alley to his bed. She looked away as they undressed him. Then the physician came in, and they finally left the Murray house.

When they returned home, Betty went to her room and curled up upon her bed. Her mind was clouded with Thomas's bruised and battered face.

And when she cried out, her father came in to comfort her.

"I will push the passage back to the next ship, Betty, so you can see your dear Mr. Murray recover."

She knew her father didn't want to say that if he did not recover she could say a proper goodbye. But he didn't have to. Tears stung her eyes at the thought. She pushed them away, resolved to praying and hoping. God would not take him, surely, he was a good person. The best man, aside from her own father, that she had ever known.

"Does he know your designs on him, Betty?"

She shook her head. "And he never will, Father. Why would I set him up for such heartbreak? And besides, his mother wants him to marry into wealth. It was not destined, Father."

Her father gently set her away from him and met her eyes. "You will find another man to marry, sweet girl."

His words stung, zapping her with the cruel truth of it. She glanced away, focusing on the red dress taunting her from the corner of her room. It had been the dress that would secure her a husband, instead it had secured Thomas's fate.

She did not simply wish to marry another man. She wished to marry Thomas. "I will not. I will never marry, Father. I will forever be under Aunt Tilda's roof. I will care for her children, and then for you, and then for her, and then I will be too old to be any man's choice of wife. If I marry at all, Father, it will not be for love. Just as you are choosing to do now. Did you love my mother?" She looked up at her father's weary eyes.

"Yes, Betty. I loved her very much. She was every thing I was not. She was every thing I needed, but knew not that I needed."

Betty soaked in his answer. She had only the faintest memories of her mother. She could remember the color of her hair, as dark as her own. And her warmth. Her face had faded over the years, but her laugh remained etched in her memory. Her mother and father would laugh often. And kiss. Betty reached out and took her father's hand.

"Father, you should not marry but for love."

Something softened in his gaze and he leaned down and pressed a kiss onto her forehead. "Sleep, Betty. We shall go see your Thomas in the morning before I must go off to accept the new goods at the dock, and beg we delay our departure."

"Thank you, Father."

Chapter Eighteen

The next morning, Betty and her father had not even reached the Murray's front door when it swung open. Mrs. Murray's eyes were pained and tortured. It seemed she had not slept at all.

"Miss Paca. Thomas has been calling for you all evening. Please, come sit with him." She glanced at Betty's father as she took ahold of Betty's hand and pulled her over the threshold. "I hope she does not have any other obligations that would take her away?" Poor Mrs. Murray seemed so very close to tears.

Her father shook his head. "Nay. Though I require she be accompanied if she is to leave your charge."

Mrs. Murray nodded. "But of course. Considering what has happened, I would not dream of sending her away without an escort. Thank you... and good day, Mr. Paca."

He nodded turned away as Mrs. Murray closed the door. Betty's mind was a jumble of confusion. Thomas had been calling out for her? Why?

"Miss Paca I am sure this is all my doing."

Betty's confusion doubled. "I do not understand, Mrs. Murray."

"Thomas overheard our conversation. After you departed, he grew quite angry and departed not much later. He was working late at his office because of me. He should not have been there. He should have been at the ball with the rest of us." She led Betty above stairs to Thomas's room. Betty stood in the doorway, staring in. She did not belong here. Grabbing her cape for safety, she pulled it around herself. Thomas had found out then, that she had deceived him. The friendship they had was likely over. How could he trust her now? Her fists balled up under the rough, brown, cotton fabric. She did not deserve to be here... he would not wish to hear her if he had a choice in the matter.

"Mrs. Murray, I should not be here."

"Nonsense. The only word he has spoken has been your name." Mrs. Murray took her hand and pulled Betty closer, desperation in her voice and eyes. "Please, Miss Paca. I will pay you handsomely..."

Betty removed her cloak and let it fall on a chair. She shook her head at Thomas's mother. "I will not accept payment from you, Mrs. Murray. I did not come here for that. I came to be assured that he will survive." She made the mistake of glancing down at Thomas. Her heart squeezed with sorrow. With his mother in the room she did not think it proper to be touching him, so she stayed aside the bed. He did not look any better in the daylight. If anything, the harsh sun's rays made him appear even worse, for one could see just how yellow, blue, and purple his skin was. Every gash was brightly displayed.

"What did the doctor say?" Betty asked softly as she stood beside Mrs. Murray and stared down at Thomas.

"He said he has four broken ribs and was beat about the head so much he is not sure if our Thomas will be of sound mind when he wakes... *if* he wakes. But Thomas is speaking and that is encouraging." Mrs. Murray took Betty's hand and held it tightly as she pressed a handkerchief to her lips. "I do not know what I would do if I lost both my son and my husband."

Betty squeezed her hand tightly, her eyes watering on their own. "Fear not, Madam. Your son is strong. He will recover."

"I certainly hope so."

Despite feeling as if she should not be standing in Thomas's room, she could not bring herself to leave. "Go lie down for a few hours, Madam. I will sit with him and fetch you at once if anything of note occurs."

"Anything of note at all?"

Betty nodded. "Of course. You have my word."

Mrs. Murray released Betty's hand and went to her son's side. She smoothed back his hair with a fingertip and pressed a kiss to his forehead. His breathing was ragged, it did not hitch or smooth under his mother's affection.

Mrs. Murray came to Betty and took her hands in her own. Her eyes were puffy and red. Her nose matched. "I may have misjudged you, Betty Paca. Had you not found my Thomas he surely would have perished. I am so sorry for the way I treated you."

Betty smiled softly and nodded. Her heart was warming at the kind words. "You have been more kind than others. You did offer me help when I needed it."

"And I shall pay you, Betty, every cent that I promised you. You did not find Thomas a wife, but you have saved his life. Thank you." She gave Betty's hands one more squeeze before leaving the room.

Betty waited until there was soft click of the door before moving closer to Thomas. She knelt down at his bedside and gently took his hand in hers. "I am so very sorry, Thomas." It was all she could speak before she broke into tears. She felt the guilt so strongly about what had happened to him. He was laying there because of her. If she hadn't initiated a relationship with Francis, this would not have happened. Thomas would be walking around, probably arm in arm with Charlotte.

Her tears would not help him recover. Her tears would not bring justice or light to what happened. She knew there was only one way she was going to find peace with what happened to him. But for now, she was here with Thomas though she wasn't sure how long it would last before his mother saw her away again. During the few hours she had him, she was going to talk to him, sing to him, do anything she could think of to let him know he was not alone.

Betty stood up quickly when she heard the door to Thomas's bedroom open a few hours later. She wiped her hands on her apron and clasped them demurely in front of her.

"Betty, has he woken at all?" Mrs. Murray asked as she entered the room. She appeared no more rested, the darkness was still beneath her eyes, but her hair was in its proper place once again.

She shook her head. "No, Madam. He has said not a word."

Mrs. Murray pressed her handkerchief to her

cheek and shook her head. Her face crunched up with worry. "Perhaps he is dying."

"No, Madam. If you listen closely, you will hear less struggle. Tis a good omen. I should leave now." She grabbed her cloak from the chair and hugged it tightly against her chest.

Mrs. Murray's fingers grasped the end of the cape, holding Betty in place. There was silence in the room aside from the ticking of the clock over the fireplace. "Will you consider staying?"

Betty contemplated the offer for a moment. If Mrs. Murray wished her to stay, she certainly would. For Thomas, her friend. He would no doubt wish for her to comfort his mother, even if they had left each other last in a disagreement. "If you wish it, Madam."

"Please. I feel safer knowing he has you watching over him."

It was many days of the same: speaking with Thomas, watching for changes, praying he would pull through. The days had passed slowly, though a little faster once Mrs. Murray handed Betty a well-worn book from Thomas's personal library. Betty inspected it carefully and opened the front cover. "What is this?" she asked as she admired the beautiful binding.

"Thomas's favorite book. He must have read it at least half a dozen times every winter. I thought perhaps it might stir him into waking."

Betty had never heard of Gulliver's Travels, but it quickly grabbed her attention as she started to read it aloud to him. Once she had reached the fourth chapter, Betty's eyes were hardly able to stay open, and soon she'd fallen asleep in her chair, the book sprawled across her lap.

Mrs. Murray came in shortly after the sun rose and placed a hand on Betty's shoulder. "Betty, there is a guest bed down the hall, please lie down, and rest for a while. Or I can have the carriage take you to your home to rest. I can call for you if he changes."

Betty slowly rose from her seat. "A bed sounds lovely. Thank you, Mrs. Murray."

Mrs. Murray's hand fell from Betty's back as she walked away. Betty moved down the hall and, with still sleepy eyes, she moved into the first open door she came upon. She gasped softly when she heard an unfamiliar male voice. Her eyes quickly widened and she tried to turn around to retreat but the voice called her back.

"Please, do not leave yet. Are you the beautiful Betty my son spoke to me of?"

She paused by the door, slowly turning when the man in the bed chuckled. "Mr. Murray," she said, when his words unfurled in her brain. She curtsied to him and nearly fell over when she rose. She was dizzy with lack of proper sleep.

"Mrs. Murray has told me you have kept a great watch of him. She must have sent you away to sleep." Mr. Murray lifted a hand and pointed towards the doorway when a coughing fit took over his body. He held a handkerchief to his mouth and when it was over, he pulled it away and Betty saw the droplets of blood left there. "The spare room is across the hall, Miss Paca. I do hope you will find it to your liking."

"Yes, sir. I am sure it will be more than ample and far above my own bed at home."

"A better bed is not truly the best, until it can be called your own."

She nodded politely at that. She had never known any other bed save for her own. "Twas a pleasure to meet you, Mr. Murray."

"And you, Miss Paca."

She was walking across the hall when she heard another coughing fit and the light but quick footsteps of someone going into his room. She shut the large oak door of the bedroom behind her, closed the curtains, and climbed into the mahogany bed.

When she woke, she did not recall her dark hair

hitting the pillow. The smell of warm stew roused her from sleep. The maid was heading to the curtains as Betty stirred, the fluffy covers crumpled, but still protecting the sheets beneath her. She was shocked to see the darkness beyond the glass—she'd never slept the whole day away.

When the maid heard Betty getting up from her bed she turned. "Mr. Thomas has come around, Miss Paca. He has asked after you."

Betty turned up the lamp on her bedside table and fixed her hair as she stared at her reflection. The maid approached from behind and gently stilled her hands. "Let me assist you, Miss Paca." The maid's hands were quick and sure. Once she was finished, she sat Betty back onto the bed and pulled the tray onto her lap. "Eat, and then you shall be allowed to see him. Mrs. Murray's orders."

Betty was ravenous and could only eat a little before her stomach started to revolt. "Thank you for your kindness. I will eat more in a bit. I would like to see him now."

The maid cleared away her tray and led the way towards Thomas's room. She stood in the doorway for a long moment as she took in the sight of him. His coloring was much better, though not nearly as pink as it ought to be, and the swelling on his face had gone down considerably. His mother sat at his bedside as Thomas lifted his own spoon to his mouth.

"Are you sure I cannot assist you?" his mother asked. She was sitting on the edge of her seat, her hands clasped tightly in her lap.

"I am sure, Mother," he said, disgruntled. "I can lift my own spoon to my lips. I do not require assistance. I am not completely..." His words cut off as his eyes clashed with Betty's.

Something stirred in her chest, an unease about standing there in his doorway. Was he pleased to see her or upset? She could not tell.

"Useless," he finished.

Mrs. Murray's eyes met with Betty as well. "I should go check on your father. He enjoys it when his wife waits on him hand and foot." She stood up, tucking a cloth napkin into Thomas's shirt.

"He does not," Thomas said, his voice thick with nonuse.

When Mrs. Murray left the room, throwing a hand up to silence her son on the way, Betty stepped in.

"Close the door," Thomas said.

"But—"

"Close it."

She pressed her lips together and turned around, pushing the door closed until she heard the click in the doorframe. Her heart was beating, getting ahead of itself, no doubt. She turned back around and slowly approached him.

"You were nearly dead," Betty said, softly.

"So my mother tells me."

"Beaten and left behind a tavern."

His eyes did not leave her.

"Thomas, why did they do it?" she asked as she sat down on the chair his mother had just vacated.

"Why indeed. Perhaps I looked to have plenty of coin in my pockets."

"Did you? Were you robbed?"

"Betty, it does not matter."

Betty could not hide the confusion from her face. "You will not be pressing charges against those who did you harm?"

"Yes, I will. But first I wish to discuss something with you." He nodded to the chair she'd often sat in to read to him. "Sit."

She stared at the chair for a moment and then did as he bid. Her mind was a jumble, wondering still how he was feeling.

"Betty, I overheard you and my mother that evening at the ball." She opened her mouth to defend herself, but he shook his head. "I want you to know I am not angry with you. I sent you to her with the confidence she would find a suitable task for you to complete. I was misguided."

Her gaze dropped to her hands, which were twisting in her light brown skirts. "I am so very sorry for even considering the idea, Thomas. I did think I had the perfect wife for you however, and it seemed I happened to choose correctly."

He was silent for a long moment. And then he asked, "Are you still leaving Williamsburg?"

She had been so busy with worry and caring for Thomas, she had not even considered her father or his plans. Slowly she met his eyes and nodded. "I have no reason to believe we will not be."

"Why are you here, Betty?" he asked, his eyes seeming to look beyond her own, into her heart.

"I..." She closed her mouth promptly and looked away. She could tell him the truth, that she was there because she cared for him. But it would not change her fate, and would only cause Thomas discomfort when he had to tell her the feelings she had for him were not returned. Instead she waited, and when he said nothing else, she looked up. He was once again attempting the spoon.

He winced in pain when his hand rose to his chest. She rolled her eyes and moved closer, taking the spoon and his soup from his hands. "Before you scold me as you have done to your mother, I know you are not useless. You are very useful to many and that is why I will feed you so that you may save your strength to heal yourself."

His steely eyes met hers and though she saw the argument swarming in his head, he only nodded and accepted her help.

Chapter Nineteen

Thomas made sure he did not change the tempo of his breathing as he opened his eyes a slit. Betty was sitting in chair beside his bed, her arms weighted down with sleep, head dropped over the neck of the chair she was sitting in. Even in this awkward state she was beautiful, her face relaxed, not a care in the world to ruffle up her features.

And yet he missed them. He missed the way her nose crumpled up when she was displeased with something. He missed the way one corner of her mouth would quirk up when she thought something amusing.

She had stayed with him for two days, two glorious days where the pain was abated by the mere presence of her in the room. They talked of literature, traveling, politics, and dreams. He had known she was a deep soul, a caring woman, who put those less fortunate above herself. She saw every person as her equal, no matter how poor or how tarnished their souls had become from the trials of life. What he could not have known was just how soothing she was to his being.

He was afraid he was going to lose her to England. He was afraid he would have to choose between Betty and his parents. He did not want to have to choose, but if he must, he knew what he wished for his future. It was not a life filled with a dark haired woman who knew exactly how to behave well in every social situation. He wanted the ebony haired beauty who might offend half of Williamsburg without meaning to. He would enjoy trying to charm his way out of it.

Thomas turned his head away slowly as his mother entered the room. There were whispers beside him, unintelligible from his position, and then a light set of footsteps left. He knew it was Betty retreating. When he heard the door close gently, he pretended to wake and turned his head back to his mother.

"Hello, Mother," he said. "What time is it?" His eyes moved to the curtains, he could see the sun peeking through the creases.

"Tis almost time to break your fast," she said,

smiling at him as if she were at her happiest while looking upon his face.

"Good." Thomas winced as he struggled to sit up. Once he was settled, back against more pillows his mother had stuffed behind his back, he ran a hand through his hair. "Mother, I have something I wish to discuss with you."

"Yes?" she asked, her attention now focused on him.

"I know you and Father have been waiting for me to choose a woman to be my bride." He paused but she did not interrupt. "I do not know if you will find my choice in bride acceptable."

"Thomas, I have no doubt you will make the right choice. You have a terrific head on your shoulders and you love this family. There is no one you could love who would destroy this family, or what we've built for you and our grandchildren."

His throat closed up at her choice of words. Was she warning him off of Betty? Did she know the feelings he harbored for her? Or was there no underlying meaning beneath her words? He swallowed back his trepidation. "Mother, if she will accept, I would like to ask for Betty Paca's hand in marriage. I know she does not bring a dowry to our pockets, but she does have much she can contribute to our estate. Her baking is exceptional. She could teach our cook many things. She is hard working, and she knows how to carry herself like a lady. It would not be that great a stretch for her to go from her station in the middling class to ours. She is agreeable to reading, balls, societal niceties..." He paused as he watched his mother closely.

She puckered her lips and then smoothed them out, her hands clenched and unclenched. When tears started to form in her eyes, he was sure he'd made the wrong choice in confiding in her. He wondered if he'd disappointed her. It wouldn't keep him from asking Betty to marry him, but perhaps he would have to make her a different offer if his parents chose not to share their assets with him. He'd already let Betty know he did not have money of his own, he was sure she wouldn't be terribly disappointed... or perhaps she would.

"Thomas..."

He looked away and shook his head. "If you and Father do not approve, I will move out at once. I am sure I can rent the room above the office for a small fee, and am equally sure if she returns my feelings, she will gladly start a life there with me."

"Thomas, please look at me," she said. He did as she bid, and her lips turned up into a smile, the tears still threatening to fall from her eyes. "Your father and I both think Miss Paca would make an excellent wife for you, Thomas. We were not sure of her intentions until you were ill, but we see now that she is no more infatuated with your wealth, than you are with her lack of wealth."

"Why then are you on the verge of tears?"

"I'm just so happy, Thomas. I am happy you have already found a woman to love you. Happy your father will be able to hold his grandchild before he goes to join the Lord."

Thomas scoffed. "Mother, do not put the carriage before the horse. Perhaps Betty does not want children."

His mother lifted her chin. "She does. A house full of them. As many as her husband can provide for."

"And how do you know such a thing?"

"We have spoken, Thomas. She does not take her meals with you. She takes them with me. And she leaves time to read to your father while I come speak with you."

The feelings he felt for Betty only deepened, hearing of her kindness towards his father. "Is that so?"

"Tis. When are you going to ask for her hand?"

"As soon as I am able to procure the perfect token of my affection," he said.

"Miss Paca, you have a visitor in the sitting room," the maid, poking her head into Mr. Murray's bedroom.

"Do not read ahead without me, Mr. Murray," Betty said with a smile as she set down a book of poetry. She gathered her skirts and left the room. As she stepped into the sitting room a pair of familiar eyes rose to greet her.

"Betty. I am glad you are well." Her father rose and closed the distance, scooping her up in a hug when she was within reach.

"Father, of course I am well. How else would I be?" She returned the hug and they sat together when he let her go.

"You have not been home in a fortnight, I was beginning to suspect perhaps you had been kidnapped."

She smiled softly. "Tis kind of you to worry, Father. I have been here, watching after Mr. Murray. He woke and is recovering quickly."

Her father sat back and sighed heavily, the sound coming out as if a huge weight lifted from his chest. "So Mr. Murray will live."

She nodded, smiling broadly.

He nodded again as he buttoned up his coat. "It seems we can leave on today's ship then."

Her smile quickly faded. "What?"

"I pushed back our passage so you could see him recovered. He is recovering. Our ship leaves the port tonight. You still have a few hours to pack your things, and perhaps enough time to see to it that the animal has a safe place to sleep." Her father stood up and pulled out his pocket watch. As he put it away, he moved to the door. When he realized that she was not following him, he turned around. "Betty?"

She stood and clasped her hands in front of her apron. "Father, I'm not ready to leave yet. Can you please procure passage on the next ship?"

"No, Betty. It was very difficult having the passage pushed back. I've been laboring day and night as a result. The passage is paid for, and that man is going to recover. I will allow you ten minutes to say your goodbyes and then we must leave."

"I—"

He grunted and shook his head. "Betty, do not tell me you are not coming with me. Do not make me out to be the villain, Betty. This is what we must do."

She pressed her lips together to keep them from trembling with her agony. He expected her to go upstairs and say goodbye to Thomas. Did he not know that in the past fortnight she had come to care for him? Nay, *love* him. Yes, she could finally admit it to herself. She loved Thomas Murray. She loved how serious he was most of the time. She loved how he protected her, and fought for others when they could not. He was brave, and strong, and so very handsome that when she stared at him it hurt her heart. Her father was not asking her, he was telling her. It was time to leave him.

She nodded and moved towards the front door. He followed after her, and as they walked he cleared his throat. "Betty, did you not wish to say goodbye?"

She sniffled and kept her eyes down. "No, Father." The truth was she would not be able to utter the words. The last time she'd spoken goodbye was to her mother, just after she'd taken her final breath. She refused to believe she would never see Thomas again.

Once home she quickly packed her trunk. It didn't take her very long, and when she was done, she sat down on the chair in the corner of her room and scooped up Mr. Blue Bell as he came purring and rubbing against her skirts.

She nuzzled his fur with her nose, then pulled him away and cradled him against her chest when her tears started to fall. "Mr. Blue Bell," she said, her voice wobbly with emotion. "I am sailing away to England tonight. Tis quite sudden, I know, but I know you will have a better home with my dear friend Sally. She will take care of you and feed you only the finest fish. She does love fish, maybe even more than you." Betty pressed the back of her hand to her lips as she tried to push down the pain. Once she had control she went below stairs.

"Where are you taking the cat?" her father inquired.

"I am taking her to Sally's, Father. She is the only one I trust with his health."

The walk home from Sally's seemed like the longest of her life. Sally had been shocked by her news, and they'd both cried while embracing for what seemed to be hours. Betty had made the mistake of looking back as she walked away and saw Mr. Blue Bell in the window. His eyes seemed to ask where she was going and why he was not allowed to go as well. She was glad he could not speak, for she did not truly know the answer.

"Mother!" Thomas bellowed. He'd been waiting for Betty to return and had not heard a single thing since his mother left his room hours ago.

She did not appear, but Joan, the maid, poked her head into the doorway. "Yes, Mr. Murray?"

"I did not call for you. I called for my mother!" The maid's eyes widened at his tone. He released a long sigh and shook his head. "I am truly sorry. I am not upset with you. Have you seen Miss Paca? Is she sleeping?"

"No, Mr. Murray. She left the house this morning."

"Is she running errands?"

"No, sir. She left with her father."

"Oh." He felt a stab of disappointment that she would not be returning soon. "Did she mention when she would return?"

"No, sir," she said, her gaze avoiding his.

He narrowed his eyes. "You are hiding something."

She shook her head.

"Joan, tell me what you know." She glanced over her shoulder and departed the room quickly. "Joan! Come back here, I was not done speaking with you!"

His mother entered the room and he sat back,

huffing loudly. He would not tattle to his mother like a five-year-old child, but he would have to speak with Joan at some point in the near future about her behavior.

"Son, you should not speak as if the house were burning down. What is the matter?"

"Betty has left. Do you know when she will be returning?"

She came over to his bedside and grabbed his hand. She held it between hers and kissed the back of it. "Thomas..."

He squeezed his mother's hand, something in his gut reacting to the way she said his name. "What is it?"

"Betty is leaving for England."

"I know," he said. "Her father is going to try to take her to England soon. That is why I thought it apt to mention my feelings for Betty so it would not be a surprise to you when I took her hand."

"Thomas, she is not leaving soon. She is leaving tonight. Joan overheard her and her father in the parlor."

His face paled as he stared at her. He pulled his hand away, and reached for the corner of his covers. With a loud growl, he twisted his body around until his feet touched the cool wood floor.

"Thomas! What are you doing?"

"She cannot leave, Mother."

"Thomas! You cannot leave this house. You are still healing!"

"Healing can wait! I can't let her leave!"

His mother put her hands up, but stood by while he attempted to rise. It hurt so badly he saw spots of bright lights in his vision, but with determination, he put one foot in front of the other.

"Thomas, at least let me get you dressed. You will ruin both of your reputations if you walk about Williamsburg in nothing but your night clothes."

He made it as far as the chair beside the fireplace before he collapsed again. His breathing was labored, and the pain was so great he barely noticed when his mother started to put his clothes upon him. She started with his shirt and by the time she reached his shoes, he was able to see once again.

"Get the carriage, Mother. I am going to the docks."

She stood, her face pale with worry, her hands wringing the apron covering her skirts. "Thomas, I still do not think you should go. Let me go for you. Let me talk with Mr. Paca on your behalf."

"No," he said. He rumbled as loud as a bear as he rose once again and headed for the stairs.

"Please be careful, Thomas."

He would have laughed if it would not have

caused him more pain to do so. Being careful is what had him in this predicament to begin with. If he had been reckless, and asked for Betty's hand the moment he came back to town, she might be staying in his bed beside him, instead of packing her possessions. If he had been more reckless, perhaps he would have beaten Francis Garrett so badly his henchmen wouldn't have attacked him to begin with.

"Tis too late for that, Mother."

There were shuffles of feet in the hallway, and his mother's gasp pulled his attention. His father was standing there, shaking hands on the railing as he stared at Thomas. "Leave him alone, Helen. He is a man now."

"A man! How is that relevant?"

"Leave him be and stop smothering him."

"I am not smothering him. Am I smothering you?"

He grit his teeth together tightly. He did not have time for his parents squabbling. One foot at a time, he descended the stairs, one hand on the railing, the other wrapped around his side for support.

He did not rest until he was inside the carriage. "We have one stop to make before the docks," he said as he laid his head back and gathered his strength. He was going to need it.

Chapter Twenty

Betty stood at the edge of the road and looked upon the docks. She stared at the ship that swayed softly. The ship that was going to take her to England. She wasn't sure she would actually accept her fate until it were staring her in the face. She hoped at any moment she would wake and it would turn out to all be a horrible dream.

"Move aside," her father said as he came up behind her, Betty's trunk on his back. She watched as her things traveled to the ship. Everything she owned was moving forward and yet all she wanted to do was go back. She wanted to turn around and run back to Thomas. She would live among the forest animals and take her chances with them, rather than climb aboard that ship and chance never seeing Thomas again.

Her father came back after handing off her trunk,

and held his hand out to her. "Come along, Betty, tis time. We must get inside and get settled."

She stood there frozen, staring at his outstretched hand. "I do not think I can go, Father."

"Betty. I will haul you aboard the ship if that is what is required. Mark my words."

She met his eyes and frowned. "Then that is what you must do, Father. I cannot make my feet move."

He sighed and rolled his eyes. "Must you be so dramatic, Betty? And must you make me jump through hoops? You were not nearly as stubborn as a child. I thought myself lucky. I am rethinking my luck." He approached her and with a grunt, he bent down and wrapped his arms around her legs. He hitched her over his shoulder and started walking with her down to the docks.

She was shocked to be upside down, and the water was so near she was sure she would fall into the dark depths. "Father! Put me down!"

"Will you walk this time?"

"Yes."

He stopped and put her back onto her feet. Her arms flailed wildly but as she started to fall backwards her father caught her. "No, no. Your clothes are stowed away in the belly of the ship, Betty. You won't fall into the water. You will smell of fish the whole trip."

She glanced at the ship and then to her father. She had to plead to him one last time. She had everything to lose. "Please, Father. Please reconsider."

"Tis done. Stop wallowing and get aboard the ship."

She stared up at the sky, wishing it would open up and swallow her. When nothing happened, she nodded and turned, heading for the ship. All was not lost she supposed, she would still write to Thomas. She would be sure he would not forget her, and perhaps when she'd saved enough she would come back to the colonies all on her own.

She climbed aboard the ship, pausing at the last step to admire the bustling hardworking people she saw loading and unloading crops and goods from a neighboring ship. She inhaled the air and stepped inside, finally accepting her fate.

The carriage came to a halt and Thomas cursed under his breath at the pain that ripped through his middle. With a hand on his injury, he waited for the door of the carriage to open. The driver reached up, offering a hand, and while Thomas did not wish to take it, he did. He needed as much strength as he had to combat the bad luck that had been bestowed upon him lately.

First was Francis. Francis and his sick opportunistic mind. Thomas knew he and his mother had killed Mr. Purcell. Francis knew he knew. Hence the beating he received because he'd come too close to proving Francis and his mother had been involved with the murder that poor Mrs. Purcell had hung for while Thomas was unconscious in his bed.

Second had been Mr. Paca's drive and determination to return to England as soon as he possibly could. If only he had made the decision at the end of the season, Thomas may have been able to do this thing right. As it were, Thomas was rushing the order of things. It was not that uncommon, but it was usually reserved for emergency situations. Of course he could think of nothing more urgent than his potential wife leaving the colonies.

A more sensible man probably would have waited until he was healed. A more sensible man would've sailed across the ocean, presented himself to his lady and, when the time was right, brought her back to the colonies.

But where Betty was concerned, Thomas was anything but sensible. He had let her take him to the dance floor. He had let her kiss him publicly. He had picked up a stray dirty kitten and delivered it to her, when he ought to have been working. He taken physical blows on her behalf. And he did not regret one bit of it.

He winced as he hobbled down the dock. Cargo was still being loaded on board so he was certain he was not too late. When he approached, they were removing the anchor from the ship so that it could be pushed off.

"Wait!" he called, his words ending in a groan as the pain stabbed him.

The men heard him well enough and glanced over their shoulders, dropping the anchor. They straightened as he approached, both eyeing him as if he might be holding a weapon, as if his visible handicap were a trick.

"Please, there is a woman on board. And her father. I must speak with them. I beg you..."

"The captain has ordered us to pull the ropes up. We are about to set sail. What is this about?"

Thomas's jaw twitched. It was not in his nature to lie. Unlike some of his fellow peers, he found it extremely distasteful, and even if it were not he would find it extremely hard to do. He did not possess the gift of a silver tongue. If he lied, it would be a miracle if it were taken for truth. If he told them there had been a very bad accident and a family member had been injured, they would certainly fetch

Mr. Paca and delay the ship. If he begged them to get the passengers down here so he could marry one of them, he may be laughed at.

He decided to attempt another trick of his peers, and removed a pouch full of coins and tossed it at their feet. "I beg you. Please retrieve Mr. Paca from the ship. My business with him is urgent."

The shorter, stockier man retrieved the pouch and slowly counted the coins. He looked at his partner and shrugged his broad shoulders. He looked to Thomas after they exchanged looks. "Mr. Paca, you say?"

Thomas stared at the ship's entrance, waiting for Mr. Paca to appear. He felt as if he'd been standing there for days. In reality, it had been barely half of an hour. Sweat was popping out on his brow and he wasn't sure how much longer he would be able to stand. His ribs were on fire, his body screaming at him to stop being such an idiot.

His driver came up behind him and spoke to his back. "Mr. Murray, do you wish me to stay?"

That was his way of saying he wasn't sure whomever Thomas was waiting for would ever actually show. "Yes, stay. If her father does not appear before my pain threshold has been met, then I shall need a carriage home."

Two more men to depart from the doors and then I shall retreat, he said to himself. After four departed from the ship he turned, his heart heavy, his strength depleted. He would not give up. He would find another way to reach her. He doubted the captain of the ship would let him ride along in his current condition. He would have to wait until he was well enough to sail.

It was not the end, he tried to convince himself, but his gut was telling him something else. His gut was a ball of knots that felt like they might never untwist. Thomas placed a hand on the side of the carriage and waited for assistance that never came.

"Mr. Murray," his driver said, pulling Thomas's attention towards the dock at his back. The shipmen were waving their arms wildly and an older man was coming towards him. He took a step towards the docks, and when he recognized Betty's father, he started walking towards him.

"Mr. Murray?" Mr. Paca asked as he grew closer. "What can I do for you?"

"You can give me your daughter's hand in marriage."

Mr. Paca's eyes widened, his shock apparent on

his face. "B—I beg your pardon. Betty? You wish for her hand in marriage?"

"Yes. I know this must be inexcusable timing for you, sir. And I apologize humbly about that fact. As you know, I was attacked and I was not in a position to court your daughter properly. I do not wish her to sail to England, I wish her to stay here with me. I wish to marry her."

He crossed his arms over his chest and Thomas could feel the paternal instinct to protect his daughter. Mr. Paca was not interested in giving his daughter away to a person who was not worthy. Thomas respected that.

"What is it about Betty that makes you think she will be a well suited wife to you, Mr. Murray?"

Thomas opened to his mouth and a sharp pain radiated through his middle. He put a hand to his body and groaned.

"Would you like to finish this conversation in your carriage, Mr. Murray?"

Thomas swallowed back his pride and gave Mr. Paca a nod. After they were settled into the carriage and Thomas's brow was covered with beaded sweat, he took a handkerchief and patted at it. "Betty is unlike any woman I have ever known. She is kind. She is giving. She is strong. She will not expect me to support her, Mr. Paca, though I will. I will give her everything and anything she desires that I can afford. But if I were to find myself in difficult times, as my father has found himself in, I do believe Betty will do everything in her power to support me too. The truth of it, sir, is that I am in love with your daughter. I am smitten. Completely."

After Mr. Paca's eyes scrutinized Thomas's face, his posture, and his carriage, Mr. Paca clicked his tongue and shook his head.

Thomas's gut sunk again.

Betty waited nervously, just inside the door of the ship. Her father had been called away and she was worried he may not have fully paid all of his debtors.

Or perhaps Francis was outside trying to convince her father that Betty should not leave. She started to make a list of all the reasons why she would tell her father she could not accept any kind of proposition from Francis. She could not explain it, but she was sure he had been behind Thomas's beatings. He had grabbed her in the street and threatened her. His mother was a terrible person. Any of those should be reason enough for her father to decline a proposition from Francis.

Or perhaps it was Thomas.

She scolded herself. She should not be so silly. Thomas was not on the dock waiting for her. He was at his home, healing, as he should be. And he would not come for her. He had plenty of opportunity to show interest and to ask to court.

Of course, you did not say goodbye.

She would probably regret that every day of her life. But she was not sure how she would have summoned the courage to tell him those words. She was not sure she was strong enough to keep the tears from showing her true feelings for him. She had planned to start a letter to him while sailing across the ocean.

She sucked in a deep breath and held it when her father appeared inside the door. His eyes widened in surprise, as if he'd forgotten he'd told her to wait there for him to return.

"Betty, the man on the dock wishes to see you."

The color drained from her face. "What man?"

Her father shook his head. "I think it would be best if I did not tell you. Go on."

"Father, is it Francis?"

Her father's brows furrowed deeply. "Francis Garrett? Are you hoping tis Francis Garrett on the dock?"

"No." She shook her head emphatically, her hands

gripping the apron on her dress tightly. "He is the last person I wish to see on the docks."

Her father's face relaxed and her dread slipped away. "Then you should go onto the docks. Tis not him."

Betty swallowed hard and gave a nod. She lifted a hesitant foot to take a step, but her father's arms wrapped around her. He hugged her tightly and it took her a moment to return the gesture.

"I will miss you," he whispered.

She frowned as she pulled back and studied his face. His eyes were glassier than usual. He set her away from him, and carried on his path back towards their holding area.

She stepped outside and with the help of the dock hands she disembarked the ship. Her trunk was being carried up the docks towards a carriage that was very familiar.

Her heart started racing in her chest as she stared at Thomas's driver standing aside the carriage. It did not stop, and only increased as she took each step closer towards the man she loved. She could not reach him fast enough, she hoped he was alright. Perhaps something had happened? What if he wasn't inside the carriage but it was his mother instead? Betty tried not to think, she tried only to be in the moment.

When she reached the carriage, the door swung open. Thomas was inside, his coloring was too pale, and there was a tremendous amount of sweat above his closed eyes.

"Thomas?" She glanced at the driver who kept his stoic expression, even as he nodded for her to join Thomas inside the carriage. She climbed in and sat beside him, gently taking his hand. "Thomas?" She tried again, her eyes searching his face, worry squeezing her chest. When he made no move, she leaned toward his face, turning her head just slightly to see if she could hear his breath. As she angled forward his hand slipped into her hair, sending a charge of sparks down her spine. She sucked in a hard breath as he lifted his head until his lips found hers.

They melted, their lips dancing together until he pulled away. "How was that?" he asked.

She stared at him, unable to speak at that moment. He frowned and lowered his head again, closing his mouth over hers, his control ebbing as his mouth conquered hers. His hands moved to her waist, pulling her in close to his body. He groaned in pain when she gave in and her hands curled into his jacket.

Quickly, afraid she'd hurt him, she pulled away. "Have I hurt you?"

"Was that kiss to your satisfaction?" he asked, struggling to keep upright in his seat.

She looked him over, confused. "Was that a goodbye kiss?"

His jaw twitched. "Is that what you wish it to be, Betty?"

Her heart pounded in her chest, and she struggled to speak past the strong emotions gathering in her throat. He turned his attention to the docks and gripped the side of the carriage roughly. "I apologize if I have offended you. I must have mistaken your kindness for something else."

She was about to object when he motioned to a wooden box sitting on the carriage seat across from them.

"Please take that with you, consider it a parting gift. A thank you for your aid in caring for me while I was injured."

With trembling fingers, she reached out and pulled the box onto her lap. Slowly she opened it, and could not have expected to see what was inside. "Thomas..."

"Betty," he said, stopping her from speaking as he continued to gaze out the window. "I do wish you acquire everything you dream to have. I only regret I did not have the courage to court you sooner than the minute your foot touched a departing ship."

Her fingers gently played over her mother's jewelry. She was certain she'd lost them forever. She looked up at Thomas. He looked so dejected and wounded, she ached to pull him into her arms and kiss him senseless. She set the jewelry box aside, carefully shutting the lid. She was overwhelmed with emotions. He was damaged, healing, and had come for her. He had seen her the way no one else had. He knew when she was sad, or upset, and he knew exactly how to calm her and soothe her hurt feelings. He was everything she could have wanted in a husband. And she was so undeserving of him.

Betty's eyes began to water, the image of him blurring until the tears broke free down her cheeks. He turned and grasped her hands tightly in his own. The comfort and reassurance eased her throat enough to speak. "I do not deserve you, Thomas Murray."

"Betty... what is this foolishness you speak of?"

How could he think her foolish? How did he not see it? He was so kind, honest, just. He was patient and respectful. He was handsome and capable. He was everything. "Your mother knows. I am not suited to be your wife."

His grip tightened on hers. "Stop speaking, Betty Paca." When she lifted her gaze to meet his, he was frowning at her. "It matters not what my mother thinks. It only matters what I think and what you think. Do you wish to be married, Betty? To me?"

She searched his eyes. She did, with all her heart, she did. But she would not marry him if he did not love her. She knew it was what he wanted most, he'd said as much at the ball. "How can I be sure this is what you really desire? I know how much you wish to help others and you wish for things to be just. I do not wish for you to sacrifice your happiness for me."

He moved, trying to sit on the edge of his seat, and groaned at the effort. She put a gentle hand to his chest to stop him, and turned. She swallowed hard as she lifted her gaze to meet his once more. His eyes were shimmering, and she prepared herself for his certain rejection. "Despite what you think, I would not marry a woman to keep her in the colonies, Betty."

"Why did you wait so long?"

He sighed heavily, his hands loosening in hers. "I am daft when it comes to you, Betty. I cannot speak when I am around you, all I can think of is kissing you."

A tightness settled in her belly. He often desired to kiss her? "I did not know. You are skilled at hiding your feelings."

"Tis the lawyer in me, I suppose. But, Betty, I would have kissed you sooner had I known you were no longer throwing glances at Francis Garrett. And if he is who you still desire then—"

"No!" She shook her head emphatically. "In truth I never desired Francis Garrett, I uttered his name to my friend Mary because I had just run into him on the street."

"That is disappointing."

She frowned and her heart sank. Had he been lying to her? Was all of this a ruse? Was he going to confess his true feelings now? "Why is that disappointing?"

"Had I known you had no interest in Francis Garrett, I would have continued to kiss you that evening at the ball."

Her heart stuttered and her cheeks flushed. A smile grew on her lips, the relief lifting her heart. "Would you have?"

He nodded, and then put his head back against the carriage wall. "Oh yes. I would have made an even bigger fool of myself than I had. For I love you."

"Do you?"

"Oh yes. Ever since you chopped Mary's hair clean off."

She laughed and melted her lips against his. This time he did not protest. Faintly, she heard his fist pound against the side of the carriage, signaling to the driver to take them home.

Epilogue

"Betty, your wedding ball has been fabulous. Surely everyone will be speaking of it until the end of the planting season," Sally said.

Betty smiled at the circle of friends around her. "Thank you. I could not have asked for a better collection of friends to celebrate with, nor could I have asked for a better husband."

"When shall I be expecting a friend for baby Heath?" Mary asked, rubbing her engorged belly. She and George were expecting their first child in a few months time. She did not know with certainty that it would be a boy, but she had a hunch.

"We do hope it will be soon, but I cannot make any promises," Betty said with a grin.

"So long as you are happy, Betty, that is all that really matters," Mary's sister, Anne said. Mary turned her head away from her sister, snubbing her silently, for Anne had never wished her own sister happiness.

Lydia, Sally, Charlotte, and Elizabeth all shifted uncomfortably.

"I am happy. Thank you, Anne. And I do hope all of you find your happiness too." Betty grabbed up her friends' hands and they squeezed them together.

"You know she would be in England if it were not for me," Mary insisted.

"Because you had Thomas pegged for Betty's match this whole season?" Anne asked, her voice thick with disbelief.

"If not for me, she would not have asked Thomas to dance at my ball."

"Tis true," Betty said. She had not planned on speaking of the letter, but if it had not been for the advice within, she truly would not have asked Thomas to dance. She may have been staring, pining at Francis for the few weeks she'd had left. "Mary did offer some intriguing advice on the topic of courting."

All but Anne and Mary leaned forward, eager ears tilted towards her. "What did she say?"

Mary chuckled softly. "Do not worry, ladies, in time all will be revealed."

Betty had read the letter once more the evening before the wedding. At the end, she'd been instructed to pass the letter to a friend who could use love in her life as well. She'd been given the letter after the stocking toss so she supposed she'd keep up the tradition. She was rather excited for the tradition for that reason. *And* so that she could slumber next to Thomas throughout the evening.

"Betty?"

Mrs. Murray's hand landed gently on Betty's shoulder, pulling her attention from her friends. They smiled at each other and on Mrs. Murray's nod, Betty turned to her friends and excused herself. Mrs. Murray pulled her aside. "Betty, I hope it isn't too much to ask of you, but Mr. Murray would like to have a dance."

Betty nodded. "Of course. If my husband wishes to dance I will dance."

"No, Mr. Murray's father."

Betty's shock was evident on her face, but she nodded. "Oh yes, I would be honored." Instantly she searched around the ball for Thomas's father's kind face. She smiled as she found him hobbling towards the center of the large room. Betty met him in the middle, and took up the dancing position.

"Not too fast, Betty dear."

"You are leading, Mr. Murray," she said with a smile.

"I do hope Thomas makes you as happy as you have made him."

"He does, Mr. Murray."

As they danced a rather slow waltz, they talked.

"Don't hurry with the children, Mrs. Murray. You will not get your young bodies back. You should enjoy them whilst you can."

Betty's cheeks blushed. "I am sure that we will, Mr. Murray."

When the dance ended, Betty led Mr. Murray back to Mrs. Murray. She pressed a kiss to his cheek. "Thank you very much for the dance, Mr. Murray."

They both smiled at her and it grew wider as Thomas came up behind her and took hold of her waist. "Mrs. Murray, I do hope you have not worn out your feet."

She glanced up at him. "You wish to dance?"

"Only with you," he said. He leaned down and pressed a kiss to her lips. They broke apart when Mr. Murray cleared his throat.

"Thank you for sharing your charming smile with my father, Betty."

She looked between them with a grin. "Tis never a problem, Thomas. I am happy to do it. Are we to have that dance now?"

He nodded as he pulled her onto the dance floor. As they danced, they stared into each other's eyes, their bodies singing with the barest of touches that were allowed in polite society. When the music stopped, he leaned down and whispered into her ear, "We must do the stockings now, Betty. I cannot wait much longer to kiss you properly."

She smiled. "I could not agree more. I will meet you in bed."